THE 10TH MASTER

BIG BAD MAGIC SERIES

ROSE SINCLAIR

This is a work of fiction. Names, characters, places, and incidents either are the product of the author's imagination or are used fictitiously. Any resemblance to actual persons, living or dead, events, or locales is entirely coincidental.

ISBN: 978-1-7359375-6-4
Art Over Chaos Publishing
artoverchaos.com

To my future self, you truly deserve good things.

♟

Part One: Wills and Wishes
Chapter One

All my problems started after his arrival. It's not every day that a necromancer walks into town. Actually, it's not even every week, or even every century. A mage like the Mad Hatter has never been to Agrabah. But he was there now, surrounded by a swarm of sun-rotted scorpions. The absolute worst desert critter living, or dead.

The necromancer was invited in on the arm of a royal. Autar would probably tell you everything started to go downhill for me the moment I first started drinking years ago. But, oh no, it was that sodding mage.

After first meeting him, our overly fair Princess Jasmine welcomed both him, and the runaway prince he travelled with, into her court. This resulted in me being stuck with not one but two mages under my nose for about a week and counting.

As Captain of the guard babysitting should have been below me, and yet, the two were so curiously powerful Jasmine assigned me as their protection detail as a show of respect. Not that either of them seemed particularly formidable in subduing any of us in the first place.

1

Currently, the Hatter was looking over flower arrangements for his upcoming wedding to the prince. The man next to him was equally twig-like but held himself like the aristocracy he was born into. The prince had already corrected me twice now that he abdicated his throne and that I should call him Henri instead. A request that felt too intimate to fill.

The type of love required to give up your crown, fake your death, only to sit back and smile as others chose green arrangements over pink was beyond me.

"Were you ever actually a hatter?" Autar asked. As my second in command that man really should have been doing anything else. No sense both of us attending to such trivial matters.

"A hatter's son," the mage answered, his eyes losing focus as if he was looking a great distance to see that far back. "Quite mad though. Which is a good name for me."

"Huh?" Autar asked.

"Madison, I mean."

"Ah."

"When were we?" Madison asked, tilting his head. "Oh, so I kept filling the shop with non-hats. Any magical thing that I found wonderfully queer. Somewhere between then and now, after a near affair with Time and Death I became what I am now."

Autar's laugh sounded like low thunder. How and why he's so curious about the two of them is just more proof on why we didn't work out as a couple. This duo is nothing but nonsensical, and Autar isn't even on duty right now.

I sighed, staring at Autar's broad muscular back under the guard armor as he conversed with them both until a maid stepped up to Henri asking for his presence with some other matter.

Tuning the conversation out is fairly easy, but the tradeoff is thinking about Autar's little differences from the other soldiers. Most of us have this job by lineage. Our parents explained how important of a position it was, and with a humble sense of duty, most follow suit and join.

Not Autar. I found him on the streets during a patrol on the verge of stealing something. Didn't even need the item, just claimed he was bored. Wanted something to do. There's always room in the guard for good soldiers so I convinced him to enlist.

He's got a sharp mind, and trains in the ring to be among the strongest fighters despite his body letting him down sometimes. Chronic pain was his only true foe. It only made him work harder than the others to become Jasmine's second hand before I ever foolishly convinced him to try to be something *to me* as well.

Sleeping with the men under my command was… ill-advised, although not outright forbidden. Still, Jasmine holds me to a higher standard, and for that failed venture I feared I'd end up losing much more than the title of boyfriend.

But thanks to Autar's casual acceptance that we weren't a good match, things only went back to normal, if not making the guard even better than before after knowing that.

"What's it like?" Autar asked Madison, nodding his head towards Prince Henri a way off as the maid held up various clothing choices for him. "You know… being with someone you know so well?"

For all the necromancer's lack of decorum he didn't seem to catch Autar's suggestion. Frankly, even I'm a little surprised the subject was even brought up. But I did know what Autar meant since the tips of his ears flushed red with embarrassment.

"I mean having sex," Autar blurted, as I smirked to myself.

"Oh," Madison glanced back at Henri. "Still don't know. We've chosen to wait until we are actually wed."

"Really?" Autar asked, sounding more annoyed than anything else. And for all my eavesdropping I can't figure out the why behind these questions. He'd never seemed that interested in our extracurriculars, let alone those of strangers.

"For added fun, I suppose." Madison shrugged, not seeming to care either way. A grin suddenly appeared on his face as he swayed back to slowly rake his eyes up and down Autar like he's a tree to be climbed. "Were you worried about my sex life? Or yours?"

"God no, neither," Autar groaned.

"Good," Madison bopped Autar on the nose, as he grew tenser. "I'd hate to disappoint you, already being so happy. But if you figure out what you were trying to ask let me know."

Autar could never fake a proper smile, but always tried. "I should get to work."

Madison nodded encouragingly, before stepping over to Henri and resting his head on the former prince's shoulder.

Henri turned his head to Madison with a sigh. "I told her that I don't care, everything is great and more than I need. But she keeps asking me about every tiny detail."

I thought about stepping in to save Jasmine's poor seamstress from a wayward authority who seemed incapable of deciding, when Madison lifted his head to study the offerings for half a moment. "That one with gold colored thread."

The woman bowed her head and headed back to the

sewing room to work on with the other craftsmen. Henri's shoulders droop as he shook his head. "Guess I should have just done that."

"Perhaps," Madison conceded before he kissed high on Henri's cheek. "But this way, I got to pick something that brings out your eyes."

"The staff still treats him like a prince," Autar added, seemingly deciding that he had nowhere else to be today as he stepped up next to me. "Despite not wanting to touch many of the trappings."

"They verge on the grotesque, maybe if they'd just fuck already, they'd be less lovey-dovey with each other."

Autar's eyes widened, and I realize he hadn't known I'd been listening to the while time. Then his focus shifted somewhere behind me as his lips parted.

"Hadi!"

I half expected Autar's voice, calling me crude, but broke into a cold sweat when it's higher pitch. Princess Jasmine must be standing behind me.

Shit.

Not cowering an inch, I turned to face her. Many of the Royals of Heart ruled with magic. Wielding it against others either directly, or indirectly through their servants. Not Jasmine. Her drive, power, and authority from the people comes from her belief that it is her job to serve them. And mine to serve her. "Your majesty," I said, bowing my head. "How can I help?"

"You wouldn't be harassing my guests now, would you?" Jasmine asked, as if in disbelief I could ever fail her orders. Even indirectly.

"No, your majesty."

Her keen eyes shifted to Autar, and he repeats me,

before she spoke further. "Good, because I have a request for you to come with me into town. Since Autar seems determined to work, he can take over here for today."

"As you wish, Princess." I glanced over to Autar to see if he's upset about losing his free time, but he just catches my gaze with a slight smile like I'm the one being hassled. As if Jasmine asking me by her side could be a burden. It's my honor.

♟

Chapter Two

If there was one special skill that I had that others found wonderous, is it that I can accurately scan a crowd and see who within it is drunk or otherwise high. Being a drinker myself, there're always tell-tale signs.

It's a great sense to have when your job is protection. Not because people who are out of their mind are more dangerous, just are more spontaneous, which makes crowd control harder. Jasmine being beloved by her people, and Agrabah so far from the other lands, made most things safe. All I have to do is serve as a buffer in these situations like this when we visit town.

My frame's so wide and large, and Jasmine's so slight in comparison there's no chance at being anonymous. She used to venture out without me before I had my position, and thankfully not since.

I had asked why not once before, and she answered that when her father ruled, she could go into town and see what they said about their leader. Hear things that they were too bashful to ask for.

Now as the crowned princess, she goes out to see what people *do* ask her. It's always a different answer. Often grander as if she's powerful enough to do anything anywhere. Instead of small-scale personal things you might tell a neighbor.

The air doesn't flow as freely between the buildings in the city as it does up in the castle. Causing the bazaar to hold the heavy scent of freshly cooked meats and baking breads, making me hungry no matter when I last ate.

Jasmine was always a spectacle when we walked through the market, the flowing teal of her skirts lined with beads that caught sunlight. People never wanted to miss her and so would crowd in if I didn't use my considerable size to clear a path first.

The last time we came here, Jasmine found Prince Henri and asked about the Wolf King's disappearance. The rest of Wonderland was far away, but now most of the questions were about politics.

"Don't worry," Jasmine said with a smile as she bent down to a child holding a rabbit plush. "You and your toy are safe all the way over here. If there anything you need?"

The child conferred with the stuffed animal. "Another friend?"

The mother standing behind her smiled, expression slightly strained as she placed a hand on her daughter's shoulder. "Actually, dear princess, our shipments are being delayed."

Jasmine stood up to nod towards the concerned parent. "I'll send another guard down to get all the details from you by the evening."

Most royals made the people on their lands travel to them in order to request anything. Their needs requested in private, and never publicly answered. Here Jasmine came directly to them. Costing nothing more than cut off pleasantries as their voices overlapped.

"You should be the new Queen!" Someone in the crowd shouted.

Jasmine glanced towards the voice but addressed the group as a whole with a smile. "My heart belongs here with all of you!"

Unfortunately, we returned to the castle by the early evening and now I was the off-duty one. Wished I had some other tasks to focus on while standing around with the other guards. I would have checked out the shipping issue if Jasmine hadn't already assigned others.

I'd love to claim that my focus largely rested on the necromancer because he was wandering the halls being suspicious. But it was boredom and a distrust that caused my eyes remain fixed on his path from their room to the kitchen. Mostly bringing dishes either to or from one location to the other.

Once the stars were shimmering outside, his steps had more of a dance to them despite the lack of music. "Are you high?"

Madison came to a stop at my self-elected post with a grin. "Oh yes." His eyes narrowed in on the tree on my chest, then glanced around me.

I lifted my arms as if he was looking for a loose thread of my tunic, wondering if I could spot whatever had his focus. "What are you doing?"

"Mind your business. You aren't there yet." He started to walk off, taking a new path, and looking up at the air like a spider web caught the light.

I ignored him and followed anyway. The mage dropped off a teacup, then traveled around to the throne room where Autar was posted. "Oh, this is going to be fun."

"For whom?"

Madison jumped at my words, like he didn't see me behind him the whole way. "No one," he said quickly, then frowned. "Everyone, hopefully. Someone at least, I'm sure."

"Right…" He just stared back at me as if I'm the one wasting time after asking for an audience. "What are you doing here?"

"You are off duty," Madison declared, then suddenly lifted a finger as if remembering something and turned until he faced Autar. Who also happened to be watching the oddity of his presence here. "Him, however."

"What do you want with him?" I asked, moving fast to step in between them.

"Manners," Madison said, leaning away from me. "I said I liked you before, but don't push it."

"Is that a threat?"

"Hadi," Autar snorted. "He's fine."

"Why thank you," Madison said, lying the charm on thick. When I refused to move the mage's eyes lifted to mine with a seriousness that suddenly caused a doubt about his lack of sobriety. "Maybe you should get another drink from the kitchen."

This man has cruelty in him. I know it. If only I could convince Jasmine of that fact, then we'd all be safer.

"Hadi," Autar repeated. I tired of my own name, so I stepped aside. He gave me a curious look before speaking with Madison. "What can I help you with?"

"The non-prince would like to start eating with the other non-royals," Madison said. "With you, Autar."

There's a sudden pause, and within it he glanced my direction as if willfully trying to annoy me. "And the other men serving under Jasmine's rule."

"Has your stay not been…" Autar also paused, but the hesitation is from lack of diplomatic wording. "The best we have to offer?"

"It has been," Madison answered, "and thus the problem."

"Ah, understood. I'll let the princess know of your wishes."

Madison bowed at the waist, a far more formal gesture than he'd ever given to Jasmine, which *does* makes me want to drink my irritation away. But since that would prove him correct, I stay planted where I am.

Once Madison left, I turned to Autar who had a tight expression on his face. "You going to leave, so I may do my job?"

"Yeah." The rules stated the guard on duty must never turn their back to anyone in the throne room. Meant to protect Jasmine from literally any threat. And while Autar knew I would never let harm befall her, he also knew I'd be upset if he broke any safeguard so close to her private rooms. "Of course."

Guess, I'll go to the kitchen after all…

With a bottle in my hand, I start spilling the oddity of my night to the kitchen staff. "So after leaving, no fleeing, the comforts of the Hart family, this Frog Prince now wants to eat with the guard tomorrow. Next, he'll ask you to teach him to cook."

Our baker, Ellie, laughed softly as she waited by a warm oven. "I wouldn't mind, he's very cute."

"Wait, why is he called the Frog Prince," the chef asked. He's a man named Remmi, and as large as me. But with far less muscle since his job requires him to stand around tasting things all day. I once tried to get him to enlist instead, and he snorted like a bull. Asking why he'd leave heaven just

11

to get all sweaty. I didn't have an answer for that then, or the one now, so I took another swig of my drink.

"It's because he kissed so many women," the baker added before sighing wistfully. "I sure missed out."

She was kind and had a small enough frame where I could see them together — if I wanted to lose my appetite — but I'd break him in two and his magic would spill out.

"Not sure that's how that works," the chef added, as he started mixing his dry ingredients together. Fear that I said that thought that out loud kept me silent, as he turned towards the ovens. "He's related to the old Queen, and that family is mean. I don't want him in the kingdom. *At all.* Let alone in my kitchen. What if people come for their little runaway?"

"Yes, see, exactly!" I leaned over the counter to get a better look at what is being cooked. "You aren't blinded by his looks."

"Don't dismiss me," Ellie scolded. "You aren't inherently correct to judge."

I raised a brow as I took another sip, just waiting to hear about how wrong we are. Which somehow upset her more as she tossed a hand cloth down on the counter. "Then explain the honorary title."

"Frog legs," the chef countered. "Wife also has lean legs for days."

Needed to drown that image out. "Do you do nothing but gossip in this kitchen?"

The tease wins me back Ellie's slight smile, but the chef considered the comment further. "And eat."

The baker ignored us for a moment to pull pastries out of the oven. "You need to try these, Hadi. Get some carbs in you so you don't have a hangover in the morning."

I agreed, not over the hangover, but because Ellie is the best at what she does in the whole kingdom. An army marches on their stomach and this duo are the unsung champions of the guard.

♟

Chapter Three

While made with love, the meals for the guard are made in large quantities and dished out without much further consideration. There is some variety on the table, as the plates of curry are broken up occasionally by sides of pita chips, or other flat bread variants for those who need a different diet.

Seems that our guests convinced Jasmine to also allow them to look the part this morning. If they kept at it, she might even cancel all the wedding arrangements and just have them sign a piece of paper. Might be even more poetic since the prince handled over the deeds to his land without any fanfare.

They did blend in far better, with a glance over the galley only their hoods would mark them as mages among the light sprinkling of other casters sitting with the rest of us.

When you eat three meals in the same room, with the same people around you, only their proximity to me made them stand out. Instead of being free while I ate, against my will now learned that necromancers don't need food. How something could be alive, but not consume sustenance was beyond me, but I didn't wish to know more either.

Henri gave the small mound of food on his plate a sincere effort, before the spice kicks in and his eyes started to water. A hand goes to his mouth to cover the faux pas while I do my best not to snicker at him by focusing on my own breakfast.

"Oh, that is quite hot," Madison said. I glanced up to see he'd dipped a finger into the dish and licked it off his finger to taste it for himself. "Stark change from the pancakes and bacon at the last table we shared with others."

"Pardon me, Captain," Madison said, looking up at me now. "Might you have something a bit sweeter for my sweet?"

"No." I'm barely able to hold back a groan as my stomach soured.

"Mads," Henri scolded under his breath. Maybe slumming was embarrassing. The nobility's taste palette was always skewed towards lavish tastes. But Ellie mostly bakes for Jasmine.

"Here," Autar said, before stuffing his mouth with an apple before standing up. Then proceeded to slide his own plate across the table until it's in front of Henri.

Despite not wanting to be treated any different, Henri's eyes are wide as they look down at the offering. "Thank you," he added, looking equally dumbfounded as touched by the offer. "May I ask, why is your meal different?"

Autar took a crisp bite of the apple that is blocking his mouth. "It all tastes good to me, but my insides can't handle the seasonings, so I get the left-over fruit before it goes bad. Amir, down at the end of our table, is allergic to peanuts if you have more common allergies."

The guard in question glanced towards us, before continuing on with his meal when we don't gesture him over.

"This is wonderful, thank you." Henri picked up a slice of melon that I used to tease Autar about always having, since no one else ever wanted it. Fresh fruit is saved for the dignitaries, but even Autar agreed that cantaloupe is filler.

But by the suddenly relieved expression when Henri bites in, he seemed different.

Autar just nodded like it's nothing. I know that he never eats much at once, so won't be bothered by the loss. But our guests look deeply impressed by the generosity. Maybe I should ask Jasmine for a reassignment. He's clearly their favorite. They'd listen to him without question in a pinch.

"About your people," I started, trying to hold a conversation since I'm stuck with them across from me for now. "Are they upset about you leaving?"

"My people?" Henri laughed bitterly. "My lands are the home of the untaxed elite hoarding generational wealth from the rest of Wonderland." A shadow of a frown flickered over his face. "Afraid they are your problem now."

I finished my meal in silence, wondering if I was wrong about him. Jasmine has always been the best of the Royals of Heart. She trusted Henri, if I did too, that would mean the threat isn't him. It's what he ran from…

My shifting opinions about the prince, made me put off asking for a reassignment and by afternoon I'm posted outside their room once more.

Henri stepped out of the room, just past me, until he realized where I am, clearly about to issue a command of some sort. "Excuse me, Captain? I was hoping you'd have something to keep me awake?"

"What do you mean?" Surely, he can do as he pleases without criticism of dozing off.

"Without politics, I settle down with a book and doze off. Reading only a few pages each time."

"It's because you feel safe," Madison interjected, still inside the room. I can't see him, but Henri did, eyes flickering briefly over. I don't see how any of this could be true since his presence here has brought a possible war to our doorstep.

"I told Princess Jasmine I'd help serve the kingdom," Henri explained, "And while there's nothing for me to do right now, I can't help but feel even if there was, I wouldn't be up for the task. Surely, there's some potion available for your men who are sent away on long overnight missions."

"Yeah." My own surprise limited the reply before I clear my throat and raise my chin. "I'll go get you something and be back."

Fetching what he wanted only takes a few minutes before I'm back at their door offering out a small vile.

Henri took it from me with a thanks and examined the pinkish liquid that's capped with a cork. "The whole thing?"

I nodded. "It won't cause any harm. High in caffeine, so worst it may do is upset your stomach. But plenty of my men drink them back-to-back when they need a pick-me-up."

Henri smiled, and this time I caught Madison rolling his eyes as if not believing in the problem in the first place.

"I'll be here a few more hours before my evening rounds, but you can ask anyone at the door for anything else you need."

"Of course, thank you," Henri said before excusing himself.

"What's the news, soldier?" I asked for the countless time tonight already. Everyone's on edge, but no one seems to be able to pinpoint the cause just yet.

It's possible the kitchen's gossip was just overheard, but I keep asking and checking around to see if there's anything I can do to make everyone's night better. Feel more in their control.

This time the question goes to Autar, who is the last person I tend to ask as I work my way up the ranks.

"Feeling anxious," he said, as he stood on the left side on the throne not looking worried. "Didn't eat anything else, so can't be that."

"Think we are going to get news about the Hart's movements soon?"

Autar nodded, ever so slightly. Might have been a more certain movement if not based purely on a gut feeling. But I learned to trust his instincts.

No more than a few grains of sand through an hourglass fall before members of the guard storm into the room carrying an injured man in their arms.

Amir guided the others to place the hurt guard on the cold tile floor in front of us. There's an arrow sticking out of the rib of Burhan. He has wickedly sharp vision, so is always posted on the castle's outer wall as a lookout.

"How?" I demanded.

"We don't know, sir." Amir shook his head like he isn't sure what he saw despite his haunted look. "It's like the arrow materialized out of thin air."

"The city?" Autar asked from behind me, not moving from his post.

"No reports of any attacks."

Burhan's hand squeezed my arm. "I'm sorry."

"No apologies needed," I said, squeezing back. "You are with your brothers."

"Amir," Autar commanded, "Go inform Jasmine."

Burhan watched Amir leave his side as I moved my hands to better see his wound. The thick cloth armor is covering much of wound as blood is slowly trickling up from the puncture. He might have bled out already if the damn arrow wasn't still sticking out of him.

"On three," I ordered the remaining guards who brought him in. In sync one of us pulled out the arrow, as another guard placed down a clean cloth, and third pair of hands stack on top for pressure. "Get the healer."

Jasmine arrived before the medic, sweeping her shirts clear before she lowers to the ground, lovingly brushing his hair out of his face. "You serve well, and we will see that you can continue."

"Your majesty," Burhan said, pupils wide with pain and wonder.

She pressed her forehead to his for a moment. Gaze than lifting to meet mine with an angry heat in her eyes. "Ready your men, if they want to declare war, I'll give them one."

Chapter Four

We are not a very magical kingdom. As much as I blamed them, if I wanted to stop any more senseless attacks that twisted things in ways I don't understand, I first needed to consult the escaped mages.

My anger took a hit as I stormed into room only to spot the former prince sleeping on the side couch. Long legs curled up against the arm, as his head rested on Madison's lap. The Hatter is sitting up, awake, and lovingly running a finger over a seam in Henri's clothes.

So much of the duty of being a royal's bodyguard is to see and hear without ever acknowledging that you were witness to anything. And yet, I'm still taken back to before the attack. To earlier today when we were still unsure if anything would happen. Then further back, remembering how me and Autar once were.

Except he usually had the opposite problem of not being able to fall asleep. Nights in the field when everyone else already dozed off around the fire. Leaving just us watching over our unit. Autar always looked more tired than I felt, but if I wasn't careful, I'd easily be the one to fall asleep first.

The trick to get Autar's mind to stop racing and doze off was to ease the lagging body it was trying to compensate for.

I'd rub wherever it hurt that day. Usually his neck or back. Reminded him it was my job to care for everyone in the guard however they needed.

Autar stopped letting me help after we broke up. And the bags under his eyes showed it, but his cleverness and dedication made sure nothing else did.

I shook my head, confused why I was focused so much on my ex when my friend was injured and more could be harmed if I took them into a battle I didn't understand.

"May I help you?" Madison asked, not seeing upset that I had been standing there unceremoniously frozen after marching in.

I cleared my throat quietly. My mouth felt dry, and I really wished I had time for a drink. "Didn't work, I take it?"

Madison shook his head. "His mind wants to fight old battles, but his body knows he doesn't have to anymore and needed rest."

A pang of guilt ran through my chest. I should have been asking myself what makes a prince flee from his family, instead of resenting him for seeming powerful and yet asking us for safety.

"How does that work?" I asked, and the necromancer raised a brow. Either at my curiosity or not following the thought. There was so much we both weren't telling each other. "You... being able to read the split between the mind and body."

"Ah." Madison's gaze dropped back down at Henri, as I started to wonder if his understanding of magic would make him a good medic. "Without air, oil and water can mix. It's the added breath of life – in a world that's resistant to what you are – that causes the parts to be separated."

"Seems all... one thing to me." Magic was illogical to begin with, and his metaphor a difficult mixture to understand.

My orders were to look out for them as if they were also *under* my command. But Henri *should* outrank me, and the Hatter hardly seemed to respect anyone's authority. I could convince myself I was building a rapport with them, before getting the answers I truly needed. But I knew my current line of questions was purely selfish. "Why am I... not like that?"

"Flattened, you mean?"

I nodded.

Madison waved a boney finger over me. "It's how you carry your trauma. You don't shake apart."

"Thank you."

Madison frowned.

"Is he going to be alright?"

"Better than you."

Anger bloomed inside of me. "Look if you kn—"

"Assassin?"

"What?" I glanced around the room, it still looked exactly the same. Out the window the city still sat perfectly asleep. "Wait, do you know what's happening?"

"Huh," he said in a whisper. "Guess not."

"Then how did you know there was an attack?"

"Autar's apple." Madison's focus fell away to somewhere between us, as if on something only he could see. "He had grapes last time I saw him there. Tiny splintering differences cut through old visions making change. Archer?"

"How—" My shut my mouth as quick as I had opened it. The details didn't matter. "A magical one it seems. Only the arrow was spotted before it hurt one of my men. I need to know how to prevent something like that from happening again."

"Salt."

Henri let out a small whine. If I wasn't so on edge, I would have missed it. He turned in his sleep, towards Madison who placed a protective arm around him and continued to speak.

"Continuous. On each level of the castle you wish to guard."

The protective properties of salt was common superstition here, often used with food storage. But if a mage as powerful as him believed in an old wives' tale than I could as well. At very least until I found the blighted archer themselves. "Thank you," I said, bowing before I turned to leave.

"You're very queer for your lack of magic," Madison said, making me pause. "Both of you are, really."

By the fucking stars, what the hell was he talking about now?

"Autar and you," he clarified.

I do not have the time for this right now, wasted far too much already. "Excuse me?"

"You are excused."

My fists balled up before I could stop them, but I smiled through it and left to gather all the salt in reserve.

"You're in a mood this morning," Autar said, as I stepped into the throne room to relieve him after his night shift.

Jasmine was holding her version of court right now, on the throne that was placed under a large inset skylight that made her crown appear almost glowing. But all it does this morning is aggravate my hangover from the eye strain. There's several people buzzing around her as she sees to the colossal duty of annexing land that was legally given to her without further bloodshed.

The commotion is enough I felt as if our conversation will be relatively private.

"I am not," I claimed much too late to be believed.

"Don't tell me you're still pissed because Jasmine wants you on the easiest job in the kingdom." He moved down from the dais, and if I was in the mood would've argued about the technical misstep.

But in truth, I'm too spent from staying up all night with other off duty guards pouring rings of salt all night just in case it mattered. "Wasn't planning on it."

Autar turned around before I'm fully standing where he was. Our timing being off further annoyed me, but it's hardly worth bringing up. He waits for me to say something, but I haven't the slightest idea what, so we just end up staring at each other for a moment longer.

"Right, well," Autar started, "I'm going to find myself a snack."

It's far too simple and normal with everything else going on. Our friend bleeding on the floor steps away only hours ago. "You aren't due back on duty until the sun sets," I informed, trying to be helpful.

"I know the schedule, Hadi." He sighed, a clear pause in his plan to step out. "Is it bad that I wish for more news about the other royals? All this waiting. It makes me more nervous than actually fighting."

"I feel the same way," I conceded, before a head tilt towards Jasmine. "What'd I miss?"

"Paperwork. Declarations of war. Letters to the other Royals of Heart."

"Burhan okay?"

Autar nodded. "Not to belittle the pain done, but it was an amateur shot. Someone who wanted action, not a tactical play."

"Right there with you again."

Only half of Autar's mouth rises into a smile, but it still feels like a reward. A reminder that I can support my men instead of just ordering them successfully around.

"See you at lunch after your boring shift here."

It is rather dry compared to a battle, but what I don't admit to him is that I love being this close to Jasmine. If she needs anything, I'm here as the first link in the chain to make it happen.

When my orders change to go collect Henri and Madison for Jasmine, I pull up short hearing a heated and far too curious conversation inside.

"So it is war after all?" Henri asked. It was the exact thing he first warned Jasmine about yet doesn't seem to believe himself anymore.

"Seems so."

"What do you think happens when you die forever?"

"I don't know," the Hatter answered after a pause. "I'd

like to imagine you go to a place where you can do all the things you didn't in life because you didn't make the rules."

I took step forward, but shock over the words stopped me again.

"I'd hunt down every despotic bigot and watch them realize how powerless against me forever more."

What the fuck?

I can't see either of them, but Henri must be surprised too because he doesn't speak or seem to move about the room.

"What? If you are asking me to picture nothing, I am incapable. Before my lives is easy, it's simply history. After?"

I moved in view to give Henri an out, or possibly get a better jump on a possible war criminal. But they keep going, unaware of me.

"You're still hung up on the whole squirrel hell is dog heaven thing, aren't you?"

"And that I'm causing strangers to be hurt while I sleep." Henri falls to sit on the bed. He'd be able to see me if he just looked up, but his gaze is low on the ground. "Sometimes I don't know if you're truly this a big bad magic thing, or not."

"Thing?" Madison's casual tone changes to something harsh and wounded.

"I didn't mean." Henri is quick to speak, but Madison stands up, about to leave. The prince reached for him but comes up with nothing but air. "Please, don't pull away from me."

The Hatter stilled, looking down at the man that stumbled towards his feet. Half turned, and easily capable to turn his ire on me any second.

I had no belief in fairy godmothers, deities, or forces of good that punished the evil. But, for the first time I could see how someone might mistake *this* necromancer as one. Capricious, confident, reassuring to those who had his favor.

As a pinnacle of nobility sat somewhat scared and confused in reverence before him. All while a more knowing being from higher above shifted from playful to cosmically wise. "You started this shoving match. Are you going to fault me for not pushing back?"

Henri's eyes closed as his head lowered. "No."

"What do you want from me?"

"Stay."

Another pause. Another quiet and warm shift like from the dawn to daylight. "To win your war?"

Henri shook his head. "For me. You... you make me question things. Get me to stop before simply acting out what is expected. You're good for me, please... stay. I'm sorry. All the possible death just got in my head for a second."

Madison took a half step back towards Henri, extending a hand out and tilted his love's face up. "I can help with that."

I carefully backed out of the room before I learned how. Not finishing Jasmine's request simply so I could first inform her that their vow to fight with us was quickly waning. Without her careful clever tack, they'd bolt once more.

"Don't you think they are very curious?"

I jumped at the sound of Autar's voice as he spoke from a short way down the hall as he continued his approach. "What do you mean?"

"I mean the first time I met that Hatter he said the chain of command was kinky. Yet, I haven't seen the two of them do more than chastely kiss each other. Isn't that weird?"

No, what I just saw was weird. Sex is simple. "I think it's strange you're watching them that closely."

"Come on, Hadi." Autar scoffed, his scornful expression one I rarely see any more since he still respects me enough to only use it when we are alone.

Here we go...

"First off," he started, as if in warning what will come. "Part of our job is to keep an eye on them. Second, don't pretend like you trusted those mages for an instant since that scorpion thing."

Ugh, those rotted bugs crawled over my foot.

I glanced over to the literal magical power couple as they exchanged words softer. At this distance I couldn't hear anything, but they were hand in hand once more.

Blech. Why did it feel like it would be less gross if they were playing tonsil hockey while we all ate? Autar was right, but I can't let him know that. "I'm more concerned that you're waiting for them to fuck in public."

"You're an ass," Autar added, before falling effortlessly back into business and handing me a stack of papers. "Here are the supply reports after the tip from the mother in the bazaar. Grapes were delayed, a shipment rotted before arrival." Once the papers are handed off, he stepped away to complete his next task.

"Autar, wait." *How does that Hatter keep knowing things?*

He stopped, looking back and clearly waiting for a revised order of some kind. But I felt too guilty to ask him for a single thing. "Thank you for getting these to me early."

No smile appeared, just a curt nod and he's gone again.

♟

Chapter Five

Henri picked a piece of fruit up from the shared plate. Gingerly biting into the fruit, instead of devouring it like we did with our rations at lunch beforehand. "Do you think this will work?"

"I wish I was the strawberry between your lips," Madison answered, eyes falling away from Henri with a sigh as he glanced down to the war room map. "Not a chess piece."

As vile as I found most strawberries, I didn't know which part of his comment I hate more. The fact that he was flirting with his fiancé in a room for military strategists, or that he compared the map of Wonderland to a chess board. "This isn't some game," I said, and the necromancer didn't glance up from his study of the small glass skull piece he'd been assigned. We would agree on one specific matter. He did not match the other markers on the map.

"Everything is a game," Madison said, placing the piece back down in a new position. "I don't belong on the front line. My skills are better suited to where blood has already been spilled and there's some obstruction of what is happening. Making things become..." He paused to take a

29

moment to smirk to himself. "Disheartening to anyone attacking. As if any progress they think they gained is for naught."

Henri slowly stalked around the table and paused to study the change. "Agreed. The Hart's men will largely be mercenaries or former Cards. Everyone on their side wants this venture to be a *profitable* one. They are not an army of soldiers willing to die for their way of life."

"I can keep your men fighting until you win," Madison added, as he folded his hands behind his back.

Princess Jasmine pursed her lips considering his wording. It was rather distasteful phrasing. "And what about their lives?"

"Do you desire public health or war?"

Autar scoffed, and I knew an interruption would follow. "We want every man to come home."

Madison's expression softened slightly. "Pity, for they aren't yours to keep."

"Everyone here understands the desires and realities of open conflict," I said, trying to get us all to focus on a battle plan. "Let's aim for balance here."

The mage's boney hand gestures over the war table. "Balance you have."

"Am I not to fight?" Henri asked, noting the two crown pieces next to each other at the castle. "You don't have many mages on the field. I can fight."

My gaze pulled over to him, then over to find Jasmine and her wishes. She seemed unsure, so I placed the former prince where royalty went up in the outpost with me and Jasmine's other strategists. "Better?"

"*No*," Madison said harshly.

Jasmine lifted her chin, looking more curious than anything else. "No, *what?*"

"You don't have enough mages on the field for him to go unnoticed," Madison clarified. "Henri is not to fight." The former prince opened his mouth to speak but was not given the chance. "I've only had Henri for this lifetime, if he were killed, I would slay everyone in this room for my own sense of balance."

"Do you plan on being more protective once married?" Autar asked smoothly, as I bristled at the threat.

"I do not," Madison said, before he turned to Jasmine. "May we go now?"

"Mads…" Henri seemed like was trying to reason with him.

Jasmine approved of their dismissal with a nod, and I couldn't help but have my stunned silence continue as Madison *bowed* to her before parting from the rest of us. Henri looked pale, at least until he caught me looking at him. Then his chin rose in the same manner as Jasmine had as he followed Madison out.

The princess spent most of her alone time in the inner keep comprised of an open courtyard that housed a very large tiger.

When she was younger, she considered it a cage. And she, just as trapped as the beast. Now it was her favorite place to think and get away throughout the day.

"Here are the readiness reports, majesty," I said, lifting a planter up and placing the papers down underneath so the wind wouldn't take hold before she was ready for them. The original plan was a simple box. More traditionally suitable, but cats are cats no matter the size, and Rajah enjoyed spilling them.

"The Hart's troops are along the border, blockading only the shipments they want for themselves," Jasmine said tightly, annoyance held at bay as the tiger bumped into her hand.

"May I see?" I asked.

After a nod, she led me and the tiger up the winding stairs to a room that looked over the city. Jasmine adjusted the telescope that sat there, clearly with a location already in mind.

"Take a look." The tiger near her feet gave a deep low roar in reply as she stepped back. "Not you, Rajah," she added with a laugh.

I moved to the other side of the telescope and peered into it. A weary sigh escaped me when I saw foreigners camping along our border. Their money must have made for faster travel because most did not journey as quick, or with such a sizable group all at once. There was also a strange number of flag bearers among their midst even as they waited. Most would have had one, centrally located. They had six evenly spread out.

The number alone was unusual enough. But not only did the waving that many colors make them easier to see, the sun itself would fade the fabric from being displayed all day and in spite of the lack of forward movement. "What's on their banner?" I asked, trying to change the telescoping focus. "I can see a heart, but the others?"

"Playing card suits," Jasmine answered. "A heart, spade, a diamond. Must be comprised of the Queen's old Cards, folded back into the family after the King disbanded them."

I stood up, studying the horizon with my naked eye before turning to Jasmine who surveyed the landscape with a smaller spyglass in her hands. "That guard was mostly bullies in its prime. Can't picture that they've retrained them all by now."

"Agreed," Jasmine said, "but before they were magically forced to fight. The willingness for combat, even if bribed, could have changed things."

"I'll ready a scouting team, we'll find out."

"No. I've arranged a very specific time and place for the battle. Hopefully, it will be the only one of its kind if done decisively enough."

"Majesty?" I asked, not quite following the logic of an army that RSVP'd to a fight.

"When the time is right, all I need you to do is take your men to the southern fields, push them back, enough that they hesitate. That should buy us the time needed for the other Royals of Heart to rein them in themselves."

After we set up a temporary camp along the south, I once again checked in with the extra charges traveling with us.

Henri still had an air of nobility about him as he sat in furnished tent. The idea of offering nicer lodging was that they'd be away from the others. The last thing we needed on the eve of war was any further accidental changes.

It was explained as a 'honeymoon suite' to the guard who are made to share. And I'm fairly sure it was also the reasoning Henri used to convince his *now* husband to let him join our fight in any capacity.

He might not have a title anyone, but any trained eye instinctively knew royalty whenever they saw it. Even wearing Agrabah mage armor that looked similar to mine. Less restrictive though, with a tree on the cloak's bottom edge where beaded roots reached towards the ground, instead of the embroidered version across my chest.

Suppose there was merit in him being safely somewhere else since no matter how he tried to blend in, he stood out as something noteworthy.

There was a book in Henri's hand, while Madison's head was lying in his lap this time. Bodies tucked close as if touching was an imperative. He was almost a reverse image of Henri's proper form. Casual, but feral. The type that I'd instantly pick out within a crowd as a threat to the aristocracy.

The lack of story in his own hands seemed to tip him off to my presence even sooner than most saw me coming. "Hello Hadi, have you come to be our tour guide regarding the Hart's military advances along the front?"

I'm not sure why he decided to call me by my name this time, after being regarded by title only before. Maybe the ring on his finger put him in a good mood.

"No," I said and stood up taller. "Jasmine wanted me to check in and see how you two are faring the night before the battle."

"How quaint. Jasmine's still sending the leader of her guard to see if we need anything," Madison said as he looked up towards Henri. "Isn't that a royal showing?"

"Uh huh," Henri said, interest not lifting from his book. Maybe looming danger did aid in keeping him awake. "Thank you, we're fine."

"Actually I could go for—"

"Mads," Henri interrupted the thought. "He doesn't want to be here. Let the man do his rounds and get back to tasks he cares about." Afterward the prince looked toward me with a warm smile. "Truly, this is plenty. Our presence is enough of a burden already. Thank you."

Madison grinned up at Henri, playing at some game I didn't understand. And yet... *I'm* left with the feeling of being seen. This was absolutely the one thing I didn't want to do, and the fact that it was over with was a huge relief. Now I could focus on things that actually mattered like checking the armor, horses, gunpowder, and countless other necessities that meant life or death.

During dinner, the two mages were off by themselves, both not eating tonight. But their empty seats gave me a clear view of them still within the camp. I missed my usual company that had shifted down to accommodate the extra seats and had not shuffled back.

Henri's hands are busy correcting Madison's top hat. A ridiculous accessory any day, but especially onerous to wear with a hooded cloak. They must have joked about that since they shared a laugh as Madison smoothed the matching fabric flat across Henri's shoulders.

"Who's the pervert now?" Autar asked, sliding into the seat in front of me.

"Still you."

When we dated, I'd complain he was too innocent for me, so Autar's annoyance doubled in an instant. "Would you knock it off?" His tone is harder this time, and I only now realized he was trying to be playful before. "You're such a dick."

"You're the one choosing to sit by me."

Autar got up from the table, taking his meal with him and quickly tossing the remains into the compost pile. The other men at our table looked over cautiously. This is why Autar can't ever be right. Insult *and* injury would undermine my authority. So, I just shrug it off and continue eating. Autar is allowed to voice his opinion.

Everyone goes back to finishing up their meal. As we start our rounds, I take several glances towards the horizon, lifting the spyglass up so I can make sure I'm aware of all of their troop's movements.

They look almost disproportional, despite the added detail their relative closeness now provided. Very… top heavy. Thin even. The Hart's were not known to want for anything. Surely, they had enough money to fatten their men up.

This was as organized and as civil as a battle will get. It's a miracle Jasmine even got this much out of a deal given their tactics before. But I'm realizing the Hart family is full of politicians, not bloodthirsty killers. The archer who shot Burhan, probably got fired rather than court martialed.

I'd win this battle. For him. For Jasmine. For all of Agrabah.

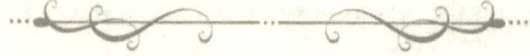

I always rallied the troops before they are dismissed for the night. It might seem counterintuitive, but I needed them content when going asleep, and eager to rise for battle in the morning.

After pacing down the line of guards gathered, I paused in the middle, inhaling fully so I could yell loud enough for everyone to hear me.

"As you dream tonight, remember this one thing!" My arm pointed an accusatory finger towards the other camp along the horizon. "They fight for riches. More gold to line their gilded portraits."

My hand moved to pound on my chest. "We fight for our country. That's what makes *us* different. United together in brotherhood. We'll be strong, like gold, but *better*.

A chorus of cheers, yells, and thumps sound off in a thunderous echo that vibrated the ground under my boots. They start to disperse, most to sleep, but some sit around the fires keeping us warm, sharing more time with each other.

Autar stepped next to me, watching them as well. "Gold," Autar said, "isn't strong."

I glanced over my shoulder at him. "What?"

"Pure gold?" He asked, as if I had forgotten my own speech and finally made eye contact. "It's a soft metal."

"Yes, well, that's why it's a metaphor."

"An incorrect one," Autar mumbled under his breath.

I turned my attention completely to him, back to the group. "Do we have a problem here?"

He rolled his eyes at me. My statue and tone doing nothing to get him to back down. "We never have a problem, Captain."

I can't stand it when he's being cryptic, so I just break off to return to my own tent for the night.

I can't sleep, so I drink, wishing it was morning. The best thing I can do to make sure my anxious eagerness for the morning doesn't spread like a cold through the others. If only there was something to do that would help me protect them all. But there's nothing besides getting sleep. The alcohol is meant to help, but it hasn't taken me yet.

Someone steps into my tent, and I know it's Autar. No one else would move with such ease. Another guard, or strategist, would announce themselves. While an enemy would try harder not to be heard.

"Can't sleep either?" I asked.

"Too hot out," he cited, before pulling off his armor.

I'm forever awed by his bare chest. Always somehow more ruggedly broad than I remember. The armor makes it easy to assume the uniform makes the man. But it's all him.

My mouth twitched with a suppressed smile. Last time anything like this happened was over a year ago. Then he claimed it was too cold as he crawled into my bed 'for the warmth'.

"Best keep undressing then." While Autar doesn't allow me to show true affection, he still occasionally accepted my boozed-up encouragement. "Better?" I asked, shivering in my own armor at the sight of him without any.

"Not yet." He stepped away from his pile of clothes, over to me, as if I needed help unfastening the only thing I ever wear.

Helping someone put on, or take off armor, has always been intimate ritual to me. This remains unconfessed, lest I ruin the careful understanding between us. "I'm so glad you drank enough to mess around tonight."

"I wasn't drinking," Autar said, as if this all is meant as a secret. "And I told you, it's *sometimes* attraction, not *no* attraction. You fucking twat."

"Thought I was a dick," I repeated, or maybe mocked. There's no difference in my tone at this point, and it's such a funny word. "*Twat*. You sound like that posh foreigner."

"Begging you to shut up before your booze filled nonsense pisses me off and it's down to none."

"I love begging." None would definitely be too little. I want more. I've always wanted more of him, so I pulled his lips to mine like he's a shot of something stronger.

Autar doesn't let me kiss for long, and even then, my tongue regretfully stays in my own mouth. But it's enough to have our hands on each other, makes it easy for him maneuver us around to how he wants, and sit on the cot together.

Every time it happens, I think about telling the same joke after he pushes my head down towards his crotch. That he does this solely so I don't say anything stupid, and unable to reach for the bottle again. And it always saved me the embarrassment of either possibility by morning.

But that doesn't ever seem true by the way he trembles the second my lips slid over his shaft and grips my long hair tight between his fingers to keep me there. I know we both need the tension we created between us to safely break before we can take on the world. He's always safe in my hands. Or rather, mouth…

Another joke comes to me as I swallowed his twitching spurts down. *Good thing I don't have a nut allergy.* I lift my head to share my amusement, enjoying myself so much I think I'm hilarious right now. But Autar is still panting, head tilted back to the slight breeze through the tent. He's so fucking beautiful that I decide against ruining the moment with a crude joke.

"Well," I said, licking my lips with a self-correction towards neutrality. "I feel better, you?"

"Definitely less pent up."

"Good," I smiled. "You should try to get some sleep

again."

Autar rubbed a hand across his face before finally standing. When we were together, he'd have kissed me again before getting dressed. This time, like the distant time before it, he just took the booze instead. "Goodnight, sir."

I frowned at the bottle in his hand, not raising my gaze above it. It's easier to pretend I'm upset about being cut off than it is to admit that I miss his pet names for me. "Goodnight."

♟

Chapter Six

In the morning, Autar prepared the troops, and frankly covered for the rotten way I felt in the morning. Thank the stars, Autar was the counterbalance that distracted me from further alcohol. I probably needed last night more than he did. It's the very reason I can't ask for anything more. The kingdom itself could suffer if I fucked things up between us.

"Units are ready and at your command," Autar barked loudly while entering the tent. To my happy surprise the volume didn't affect me at all. Ah, hair of the dog, great for hurling that hangover into the far future when I had time for it.

I took the bought time to have a moment for myself, looking over the maps once again for anything we might have missed while making the original plans.

To imagine the rival camp came all this way to do such a roundabout thing as 'protecting their home' while occupying our land and attacking our people, when the only change Jasmine made was placing her seal on a piece of paper. Was the imaginary threat of future tax really worth the bloodshed to them?

The men marched to the battlefield, the two opposing

groups making two lines and waiting for the sun to rise fully before further advancing on each other. I escorted Henri to a raised bit of land up and away from fray, where our strategists set up their tables.

The land provided no outcrop like this on the other side, allowing for only our planners to buzz around happy in their little temporary hive. Once we joined the group, I made introductions to Henri. Explaining how Jerick is our chief military strategist.

At his name, the man stops what he is doing and stepped over with a forced smile on his face. I know he's expecting some rallying speech about their hard work today. But instead, Henri just bowed a little and offered a hello.

Jerick waited an extra moment for the rest of it, then his expression softened. "Good day to you, sir," he managed to say before rushing back around and squeezing extra last seconds of extra time he was given.

The battle itself starts a little before noon because the mages on their side start a chain reaction of ours. Besides the countdown, the fight below looked like all the others had. Arrows fly first before the blows come from closer quarters.

I'm able to look at Autar and the other men with a sense of pride, knowing that we are managing and watching over them the best anyone could ever dream to achieve. Henri, however, watched with an expression that caused me to wonder if I should grab him something to throw up into.

Blood makes plenty nobles queasy, but as his jaw tightened, I recognize it's a look of the sky right before it cracked open with a storm.

Henri started to climb back down, towards the fray, and panic gripped me. "You need to stay here, where it is safe."

"I'm not a ruler in need of protection." When he turned,

his gaze caught me and his eyes were jarring. Suddenly animalistic, and full of magic. "Madison and I are leaving. We've made a mistake being here."

"Yes, sir." The reply was automatic as my mind lagged over the math. If he wasn't a royal, he couldn't give me orders. But if he was a citizen, he shouldn't be here either. *Shit.*

While my focus had been away, now a curious thing is occurring on the battlefield. The slain men are back on their feet, weapons skillfully risen and attacking again. It isn't even my men. It's all of them, on both sides, now targeting the outsiders.

In the back of the pack, I spot Madison's top hat as he glided, dodged, and even twirled around who neared. *My god.* I never imagined necromancy to be so literal or done so playfully. *Was death just a joke to him?*

As Henri approached, Madison stopped the dance, but kept his arms still low as if the magic still flowed. The dead fight, keeping them safe, but there's also more now. A heat mirage distorted the air around them. Blurred their forms as they speak.

An arrow flew through the area, the wood burned up before reaching them. *They both are powder kegs.*

With a shrug from the necromancer, the duo began to walk towards the city. Each step away from fray, the fighting corpses slow until they were simply slain once more.

"Make them to come back," Jerick suddenly said, looking quite feverish over their choice. Clearly desperate for me to do something since he left his maps. "The Hart's men will push this advantage and overpower ours. The guard doesn't yet know the mages don't have their back."

There is no way we would have gone into battle if it completely hinged on the presence of two people. "Would any backup suffice?"

"Not any." Jerick shook his head. "Yours might. They trust you."

And I trust them, so I climbed down the outcrop and joined the battle. Our two groups are fairly intermixed now. I pulled forward my sword, and worked my way slowly to the front, so if any absence is felt, it's not a fear that stays long.

Their leader, if one could bestow just a title on the man, was positioned on the remaining patch of land that is comprised of just them. Fighting, but not really.

While his decorative armor is more than capable of taking blows. The man inside it is not. He is large but shaped in a way that is all show. If he were to run, he'd quickly it winded. Let alone put up a sustained fight during it.

The stranger lifted his sword as I near, and I tossed mine to the side and let out a barely human roar. The enemy took half a step back and before his momentum even fully stopped, I body-checked him to the ground.

My fists wail on him, before another attacker made me roll off. The play-soldiers carried their icon off and away, as they start to retreat. This battle of blades quickly turns into a chase.

After my valiant entrance, it seemed I also created an opportunity for dissension in the ranks. My fallen sword is lifted up in the hand of another guard and comes to rest under the chin. A hair away from giving my beard a close shave. "Seems you dropped something."

"Autar," I breathed out like a wish, tongue darting out over my lips.

"Yes, Hadi?" The man asked with a grin. He would not touch me here, but he still could hold onto this delicate moment on the literal tip of a sword.

I swallowed hard, remembering last night. "We need to secure the perimeter."

Autar's head turned to the battlefield before us, nodding once. His wrist flicked down and around to properly offer the sword safely back to me. "Yes, Captain."

My breath caught as our fingers brushed against each other with the exchange. And I swear his doesn't.

I might have gotten a medal for my valiant morale raising efforts if the two deserters didn't return back to the castle with us.

Instead I found myself summoned to the court, representing the guard, as Henri worked on talking his way out of this while the Hatter wisely stayed silent.

"Our arrangement was for you to protect the kingdom," Jasmine said, posed with a tight annoyance on her throne.

"No, dear princess," Henri dared, instead of just bending a knee. "The arrangement was you inherit my land and possessions upon my presumed death in return for asylum here. What good does it serve any of us if we are seen fighting? Or even dying in public? We can help another way."

"Your necromancer can turn any tide of war, what better use is there for you two?"

Autar stood next to Jasmine, his focus on the other mage. Equally wise of him, since if anyone was going to break rank and threaten Jasmine, I'd place bets there.

The Royals of Heart largely use their tongues to cut each other, not weapons. But I'm too busy wondering if he liked being called 'Henri's necromancer'. I wouldn't bet my life on it, but I think he does enjoy it, and that's why neither a correction, nor an attack comes.

"You might not fully understand our nature because you're not a mage," Henri said, "but there's plenty of imaginative ways use us besides in a direct fight."

"Your guard's captain," Madison ventured, with a step forward. Autar mirrored him, ready to put himself between them. "May I ask him a question?"

Jasmine lifted her chin in caution but permitted such allowance.

"What is your goal when entering a battle?" he asked me.

If this was a riddle, I didn't understand the trick hidden within it. "Protecting the kingdom and returning with as many men as possible."

Madison waved a hand in the air. "So, preservation of life?"

"Always."

Jasmine smiled at this, and I'm filled with pride once more as my annoyance at him settled.

"I can see the future," Madison continued, "Tell you what path will yield the result you want with the least amount of death."

"You can do that?" she asked.

Something told that means she's curious to see and won't be convinced otherwise. *Great, more magic.*

The mage nodded. "Necromancy is as much about avoiding death as it is healing what has died."

"Shall I consider the terms revised?" Henri asked and held out his hand for Jasmine to shake.

Jasmine glanced at the necromancer for a moment more, judged him as truthful, and stood to take the offered hand. "If we can avoid the bloodshed of my people then I must find that path."

♟

Chapter Seven

The Hatter breathed in the magic smoke, as deep as his lungs allowed and held it until he shuttered. His eyelids fluttered before he finally exhaled and now sat there peacefully with pure white eyes.

Henri is on his left, and Autar is crouched down in front of him being one of the only guards who still trusts they care about the kingdom. I'm glad the rest of the men aren't here. So far, it has been a spectacle. Ellie came into the room to deliver a plate of baked goods several moments ago and is still in the room captivated by the pre-show.

"Hatter?" Autar asked. "Can you hear us?" There's no reply, so Autar glanced to Henri for support.

"Ask him about what you want to know," Henri prompted. "He needs specifics to focus on."

Autar nodded. "What do we need to win this war?"

Madison's body twitched like a dreaming animal before his lips parted and released more smoke. "I drive men mad for the love of me. Easily beaten, never free."

The fuck?

Ellie and Jerick tried to collectively guess, but their collective nonsense didn't get us anywhere.

"Gold," Autar guessed, sure of himself. "Do we need gold? Where do we get the gold?"

"My life can be measured in hours," Madison continued without confirmation. "I serve by being devoured. Short, I am quick. Tall, I am slow. Wind is my foe."

I crossed my arms over my chest, huffing over the fact that we traded a fighter that cannot truly be killed for a handful of word games that could be found on a playground.

"Um... Oh, I know this," Autar said, ignoring the others guessing random things. "A candle?"

Madison didn't react to this answer either, so Autar looked to Henri who at least nodded his approval. "He probably means candle's smoke. It's how my magic mirrors are powered. We'd be able to see and learn much with them. But we'd have to get there first."

Autar smiled as if they made progress instead of just wasting time. "How do we get to where we need to go fast enough?"

"Travelers I lose," the utterly out of his mind mage continued, "but shelter I offer. Upside down my company sleeps. You may find me in the sun, but within there's always darkness."

"Upside down sleeping?" Autar asked himself. "A bat?"

"Darkness within a bat doesn't make much sense," Ellie said, with a mouthful of cookie.

No one is guessing anything that makes this farce come closer to ending. With a heavy sigh, I decided to guess. "How about a cave?"

The smoked-up mage's body spasmed enough that his

top hat fell from his head. I hate seeing people like him in any type of altered state. If they lost control anything could happen. The whites rolled forward, and his now brown eyes blinked a few times.

Wait... I got the riddle?

"Stars, I hate that," Henri confessed as his husband came to.

"I'm sorry, love," Madison said softly, completely clueless about the strange show he put on. "Would it help to know what I saw?"

"Doesn't help me." Henri gestured towards me. "The information was for them."

"Ah, right you are." Madison turned his head, looking perfectly in control once more. "I saw what you need to end the war in the manner you want. There's an artifact in a timeless cave with wondrous properties able to grant the wishes of the owner. Bring this to Princess Jasmine, wish for your men to be victorious and safe, and so it shall be."

What? I scoffed. "Do you mean to tell us you had a vision of where we needed to go? Then why were you asking all those riddles?"

"I was saying riddles?"

He looked genuinely confused, and it's the main thing that keeps me from knocking his hat back off the moment he rights it.

"Yes." Autar laughed, and unfortunately covered up my huff. "Several."

"I hope they were good ones." The ancient mystic aura ended abruptly as he softly took Henri's chin his hand. "Now, what can I do for you?"

Here I thought Jasmine keeping a tiger tempted a dangerous end. Did that prince even understand what he had courted? Wed? Renounced everything in his life for? By not voicing my objection, they continued their far too sweet display.

"Simply seeing your beautiful eyes again is all I needed," Henri cooed.

"They are quite alright, aren't they?" Madison looked up as if he could see their color.

I was not going to make it through today without a drink.

"Did you guys pass the caves on your way here?" Autar asked, blessedly still focused on work.

The two looked at each other, sharing a little shake of the head.

"Wow," Autar breathed out in a hushed tone. "You really saw inside them, didn't you? There's an ancient cave system our archaeologist's study. Is it possible to tell which one we need to visit from the outside, so we don't have to search them all?"

The Mad Hatter titled his head as if listening for the answer. "It's the one you think looks like a lion's mouth."

"How did…" Autar stammered. "How did you know that?"

I grumbled, not wanting this nonsense encouraged any further. "The same way he knows anything, it's magical puffery. And that cave does *not* look like anything like an animal."

Autar rolled his eyes. He wasn't looking directly at me so he seemed to think I wouldn't notice. "What does it matter? The trip is worth it if it saves lives. I knew that cave was something special."

"Go tell Princess Jasmine the news."

Autar gave a respectful bow, then turned to fulfill my

orders.

"You know you two should only fight while outside," Madison said. "Being in such tight quarters all the time makes people claustrophobic and therefore defensive. Least that's what Alice said, and it works for us."

"You're still seeing things," I countered, holding onto my thin line of being proper. "Because we weren't fighting."

"You would have, had you not been working," Henri said. "Lion head to you, or not, you refused to concede he was right on any front."

Why didn't Ellie serve drinks? I picked up a pastry in hopes they'd get the message, yet still foolishly didn't stuff it in my mouth. "And am I meant to know who Alice is?"

"Stars!" Madison exclaimed. "I hope not. She doesn't belong in this story."

Right… "I bid you a good day, sirs." With manners out of the way, I left them with the others.

"Ready to go on your first solo mission?"

I closed my eyes, allowing myself a moment to say every cuss and negative thought in my head before I dared to open my eyes.

By the stars, they were matching today. Dressed in what could be only described as identical adventurer outfits was one former prince and one necromancer who was still talking. Least he didn't have the damn top hat today.

I scrubbed my hand down my face and took a deep breath before speaking. "Yes, yes, okay," I said quickly to get him to stop. "But how is it a solo adventure if there's three of us?"

Madison lifted a finger to count, starting with Henri, me, then himself. "Oh, I must have been thinking of something else."

I had a headache and wasn't even sure how this conversation should have started, let alone where we were now. "Let me guess, I'm escorting you and Henri to that 'wondrous' cave?"

"No," Henri said, throwing me off for a second. "Jasmine's wishes were for you and Madison to visit the cave."

Madison counted off to two on his fingers before shaking his head. "I'm qualified since I'm an expert in all things magically historical since—"

"You owned an antique shop," Autar said, finishing the sentence as he entered the room, "for 'longer than either of us have been collectively alive.' We know."

Oh. I did remember that conversation now. It started with them bringing the idea to me, and I said the Princess would never send her guard captain away during an open conflict.

To which one of them replied, 'we will see' before convincing her that she must do exactly that. At which point I silently vowed I'd get drunk enough to forget I backed myself into a corner. "Wait, why are *you* dressed like that?"

"Like what?" Autar asked, glancing down at himself. He was also wearing traveling gear, but a more practical version for the desert. It was deeply strange to see him out of uniform. Not matching every other solider in the guard made him stand out. There were short sleeves that cut off at his biceps and a scarf around his neck hid his Adam's apple.

"Just how drunk are you still?" Henri asked, rather meanly. "I asked for Autar to go with, so you wouldn't be miserable alone with Madison."

"Henri is actually the tag along here," Madison explained, before turning to look at him, voice high and near babble. "Claimed he couldn't let me go without him. Afraid you'd have your way with me."

Blech! "I'm going to throw up."

"That's not what I said!" Henri laughed. "I said you lose time too easily, and rather lose it with you."

"Oh my god. I don't fucking care," I groaned, and the room fell silent as I realized I yelled over everyone.

"Ignore him," Autar said in lieu of apologizing for me. "The sun on the way there will dry him out. His tongue is looser after drinking."

"You'd—" This time I had enough sober clarity to know I absolutely did not want to stay that thought out loud.

"That's actually very dangerous," Madison said, and if he wanted to play nurse, I would snap him in half. "Let's wait until nightfall."

"Absolutely not, I'm fine." I started to gather my things for the trip. As I left the room I called back to the group. "And I'm not changing!"

Sun and alcohol aren't so bad if you have plenty of water and something to give your skin shade. We traveled past the city on camel back until there was nothing surrounding us but dunes. Sand stretched on top of the world like a smooth golden blanket.

It would be another few hours until we reached the cave system and exactly why I wanted to leave when we did. If we started at night, it would have been too dark to travel without getting lost.

When we stopped our camels outside the cave system and dismounted, I worried the heat had gotten to me because the damn thing did look like a lion's head. Mouth open mid-roar and just waiting to shallow us whole.

"It's changed," Autar said, and took a step back to check the caves position compared to the other land markers. "This is the same spot, but… it's different."

"Once we are inside, don't touch anything besides the lamp," Madison warned. "Actually not even that before I see it."

"You saw what we are here for?" Henri asked.

"I didn't mention that before, did I? Didn't fully see it until we were here," Madison said, then held his hands out in front of him showing size. "There's a gold oil lamp about this big. With a chain attached to from the handle to the topper."

I recalled the riddle answers: Gold, candle smoke, cave. Least his constant nonsense was consistent to itself.

We stepped in using the daylight that was able to reach into the mouth of the cave. The wind also followed us in, whistling through the naturally carved out space. Despite the fanfare the outer appearance was given, inside was no different than any other cave.

Along the walls were faded dashes of paint. Took me until we almost ran out of natural light to realize they were a surveyor hash marks.

"Addendum," Madison said, pausing as there was a strike of flint as Henri lit a torch he was holding. The orange licks of color dancing around the cave until settling into a steady glow. "Don't touch anything man-made that we didn't bring ourselves."

"Looks like the path gets steeper from here on," Autar said, a short way in front of us. I could barely still see him this close to the light. His voice almost caught an echo within the chamber.

"I want to be clear here," Madison insisted. "The land is safe. Grab onto something if you need as we climb."

His seriousness at least bought my silence as Henri prepared another torch, this time offering it to me before they moved up ahead.

"Do you trust them yet?" Autar asked softly as I paused next to him. He'd stopped to overlook what I thought once might have been a waterfall. We had walked straight so the empty space now above us with protruding stalactites was rather baffling.

"He does seem... well informed."

Autar cracked a smile and started moving again, our group capped off with two torches on each end. A strategy I started to doubt since Autar and I's size was fair less nimble than the others. We seemed likely to slide into them. But changing positions might make it worse because I at least needed the extra light.

"Careful here," Madison called back. His silhouette bent over to touch the ground right near his foot. Hand on a rock he had avoided before righting himself.

We slowed so Henri could climb over without pressure. He found a balance with his head down and hands out, then paused for the rest of us on the other side.

Autar went next, kicking down a few smaller rocks along with him. He turned back to face me a couple feet below. "Toss me the torch."

I did as asked, and the shadows shifted around with the movement. As I stepped to where Madison had mentioned to be careful, my eyes lifted further up along the backwall. With their flames below, the painted scene held a campfire underneath a constellation of white dots. Powerful strokes showed figures with spears and a boar.

My throat tightened, wondering how many of our people had stood right here. Was it our fathers? Our grandfathers? How much history had we lost by not mapping out this cave system?

There was a crunch under my boot, sediment shifting over uneven crumbling rock as I slipped. My fingers dug into the ground trying to find a handhold.

Instead of staying out of the way, Autar dropped the torch and put himself in my path. Crouched down to keep his weight centered and secured one hand around a tree root while extending the other for me.

I caught it, the momentum staining our hold as I slid just passed him to a stop as we held tight. No worse for wear besides the dirt I felt between skin and clothes.

"Guess, I should have been more careful," I said, a bit embarrassed that I fucked that up, even after the warning. The mages were looking at me if I was crazy as I stood up, brushing myself off. "What? Autar counts as coming with us, and everything else was the ground."

"That he does," Madison laughed, face lit as he held a torch. "And the lack of care on the rock?"

"I got distracted by the cave painting." My head tilted up to see them again, but from this angle they sadly didn't catch the light.

Henri appeared like the only other one interested, but his attention pulled away as Autar reached for the other torch. "I got it," he said. "Maybe you two should be the middle until the grade changes again."

"And you?" Autar asked.

"Will be fine," he smiled, then glanced to me to I assume pass along the same question.

I thought of objecting, but the terrain quickly proved how right he was. The cave got tighter, my knuckles scrapped against sharp rock as I slowly pulled myself through.

When the limestone opened up again, I gulped in air, no longer feeling claustrophobic. We all seemed to naturally pause on the other side and waited for Henri. Autar brushed off the plant matter that had clung to his clothes. My leathers hadn't picked up much, but there were darker spots from the moisture on him.

Henri squeezed through without a problem but seemed to find one all the same. "Mads, what are you doing?"

I looked over to see Madison sticking his tongue out to the air before he started huffing in gulps of air. His antics stopped as a hand pulled up to his head with a grimace. "There's foul air here, we have two hours or so to get to a passage that has fresh air."

Not looking happy with his own warning, he stormed over to Henri, pausing in front of him. "May I have some air from your lungs?"

"Uh… okay?" Henri nervously stole a glance towards Autar and me before his volume dropped realizing something. "Is now really the time or place to be kissing me?"

"Yes," Madison said, and grabbed his husband's chin as he forcefully placed their mouths against each other. Henri was left dizzy after they pulled apart, hands remaining on each other for steadiness.

"Correction, we have half an hour I wasn't accounting for our smaller frames. Over there," Madison pointed to where water trickled out from a large crack in the wall. "Break that down. Now."

With the order placed, Madison turned his attention to Henri again. Pressing his forehead to him, and I strained to listen.

"Hadi!" Autar stood waiting for the help, and I forced myself to ignore them and hoped we wouldn't cause a flood in an effort to get better air.

♟

Chapter Eight

We threw our weight against the cold damp stone. Pounding against the surface and using our shoulders as battling rams. The piled stone didn't seem very thick because on the other side I could already hear bats startle.

As rocks fell forward, they took flight in a flurry up a shaft full of moonlight. I held my hand out and felt air movement here. That Mad Hatter was right again.

"We need to go down further," he said, stepping in through the opening we created. "It's not quite wondrous enough yet."

"How?" Henri asked.

The critters that called this section of cave home squeaked and scratched out of sight before skittering away all together over the sounds of our steps into the darkness of a long tunnel.

Madison picked up a pebble and dropped it into a shaft, leaning over to listen for the sound, and likely the depth. "I'm not sure how to do this safely."

"What would you normally do if you were in a situation like this?" I asked.

"Jump bodies, find someone who failed further ahead and pick up where they left off."

"Don't do that," Henri said, "This one has sentimental value to me."

"Can't you like…" I started, trying to recall what he did on the battlefield. "Temporary extend yourself?"

Madison flushed, noticeable even in the lowlight. "Henri, I believe this man is hitting on me."

"He means half possess something else, while reserving this body to come back to."

"Oh, okay." The second he was done speaking, he fainted. Henri managed to catch him in time to awkwardly fumble into a shared pile on the floor.

"Rather wish you hadn't suggest that," Henri lamented and brushed his hair out of his eyes.

"Why? If anyone can scout ahead, I'd think it would be him."

Henri nodded, before letting out a soft sigh. "He's not the best with keeping the time. We could be waiting a while."

"Least here's safe for… the living," I ventured, trying to rally the group. Maybe I could travel ahead too and between us both we'd find the lamp faster. Or at least maybe another exit.

We waited, long enough that I ended up leaning against a wall until a loud bang in the distance rung through the cave. My hand moved towards my sword wondering if bigger animals lived her. Heard a few rocks sliding then…

"This brain, I don't like it," a voice echoed up from the shaft. That's hardly the words of an attacker so I lifted my hand off my sword and squinted to better see. "Poor thing was depressed. Catch what moves, okay?"

That had to be Madison. I braced myself behind a sternum high solid rock so reaching for whatever he had couldn't send me tumbling over. The first throw missed. My fingertips just barely grazed what felt like rope. The second throw is worse on both our parts. Autar stepped over to help out our chances.

"Could you please hurry up?" the voice scolded, "I deeply want to kill myself to get out his body."

"Madison!" Henri yelled over, still on the ground with the other body passed out over his lap.

"Yes, love?"

"They are doing their best, and you're freaking me out."

"Sorry, love!"

Autar and I exchanged a glance to each other. Saying more about this awkwardness with our shared silence than we ever could have with words.

"The rope is still attached," Madison yelled up. The shadows in the shaft shifted and I realize he must be wiggling the rope from below. "I can't give you anymore, you're going to have to risk it and reach further for it."

I moved around to where the rope had been moving. Here the ground suddenly cut off, so I lie down on the ground so my reach can extend over the absolute blackness.

"I got you," Autar added, before his hands secured around my calves.

"On three," Madison prompted, before counting down. This time when he threw the rope up, I easily grabbed it and pulled it up.

"Now what?" Autar asked me.

But Madison was the one to answer. This time in his usual body as he rose from Henri's lap. "We rappel down."

"Wait," Henri said, looking pale. "The climber you were in, did he die attempting this?"

"Dehydration."

That answer made me feel relieved, but I felt bad about the reassurance. The pulley system the last traveler made wasn't the most secure. But the area between the side walls was tight enough that I could easily stop the descent by sticking my feet out as my hands never let go of the rope.

Autar went down next, followed by Henri, then Madison who then brought us into a connecting room. "That's the climber," he said, gesturing to a lump on the ground.

When the torch light reached him, the face was ashy and sunken. Now barely more than a skeleton that I was definitely glad I didn't have to see it reanimated.

"Welcome to the Cave of Wonders," Madison said with a twirl, and I could hardly fathom what the torch's light showed glimpses of. Only after he lit up the sconces did I believe my eyes.

Piles of gold vases and goblets were piled in mounds filled with coins. Stacks and stacks of them in various heights. Glittering statues watched over the piles and golden archways marked a whining path between the maze of treasures. Swords, dishware, and chests likely full of anything anyone could ever wish for filled the cavern.

"It's a shame…" I started to mumble to myself, wanting to bring full bags back to Jasmine. This could feed plenty for generations.

"That there's no water down here?" Autar interpreted within my pause. "I was just thinking the same thing. To die the richest man in the world, but not have a drop to drink." He took the water off his belt, lifting it in toast before taking a swig. Then, even more curiously wonderful than anything here, tossed the canteen onto the pile.

Autar caught me watching him, holding my gaze for a moment. "For the next person."

"Stay close," Henri said, as he backtracked to us. "The lamp must be nearby; I can hear magic singing."

I gestured for them to go first, and we walked along the path that ended at a pedestal with a lamp sitting alone on top. Madison's hands hovered around it until they slowly closed to lift it with reverence.

Madison turned, slowly coming back down the steps towards us. "Think fast," he said and tossed the lamp underhanded towards Autar.

He went to catch it, before remembering what he'd been ordered to do before and pulled back as the lamp clanked against the ground behind him.

"Why would you do that?" I scolded.

My words were greeted with a pout. "Was only having some fun. It's fine to touch. The lamp is empty."

Autar looked flushed, unsure he if made the right choice. "There's no magic left in it?"

"There's magic, but no jinn, no traps, no reason not to head back into town."

"It's still an antique," Autar grumbled to himself as he picked the lamp up, and carefully brushed the dust off. "I'd think you'd show to more care."

The mages said nothing. Attentions split between us. Madison was watching Autar with a look of approval, which was off putting enough that I glanced towards Henri to reign his husband in. But he was already watching me.

"Let's leave before we find any trouble."

It was nightfall, as we exited the cave and made quick work setting up our small tents and building a shared fire. Autar and I sat around the warmth first, the practice doing such things saving us time.

Henri finally stepped towards over to fire, looking like he was going to speak before Madison popped out of their camp. "Leave them, love. We are all tired."

"We will watch it," I said, nodding towards the lamp in a bag near Autar. "You can retire for the night. Nothing to do but rest before traveling in the morning."

He gave a practiced princely smile before ducking back under his tent.

Autar nodded towards their direction. "Quite weird tonight."

"Lost your trust in them?"

He shrugged, then glanced over to the lamp. "I feel like there's something they aren't telling us. How is a regular golden lamp meant to save our men from dying in a war?"

"You need a drink," I declared and dug through my own bag to grab my flask. After a swig, I offered it out to him.

He stared up for me for a moment, and if Henri was withholding anything from us, so was he. "Come on, only a drink."

One drink, turned into two, which turned into three. And soon we had our hands all over that lamp trying to figure it out. Far as I could tell it didn't do anything besides hold incense. Which I couldn't even try because who brought that with them when exploring a cave?

"Finish it off," Autar said, waiting to exchange the flask

for the lamp again. Wordlessly, I took that trade. "There has to be something special about it."

"Maybe…" The thought had nothing behind it, so I finished off the booze before admitting anything else. "Maybe it's lucky."

Autar smiled at this idea but didn't look convinced. "I'm going to turn in. Are you coming to bed? I can put the fire out for you."

"Not yet," I said, looking at my reflection in the lamp's surface and smirked to myself. "I'm thinking about rubbing one out first."

"Bad," Autar said, standing there above me in judgment. "That's a big bad joke."

"I quite enjoyed it."

"You would."

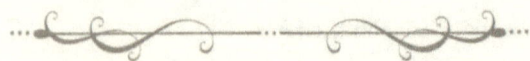

The journey back was uneventful, and I didn't even have to baby myself with drinking enough water since I didn't drink much the night before. But I was quite tired.

I had stayed up trying to remember any myth, legend, or historical fact that was related to that cave or the lamp. Anything that could make it a symbol that would encourage others towards victory and safety. But came up with nothing and before the end of the day I stood in front of Jasmine with our reclaimed treasure.

With a knee bent in front of her throne, I offered up the *somehow*-magical lamp. She rose from her seat, lifted it up from my hands with a deep respect.

"You did well. Your kingdom thanks you," she said, before turning to Burhan who standing next to her with a pillow. Carefully she set the lamp on it as if only her hands were to touch it from here on it out.

"Where is your fellow guardsmen, Autar?" Jasmine asked.

What? I looked around the room, knowing that Henri and Madison weren't here, but Autar had been right with me. I had spoken to him not more than a moment ago.

"He's… watching the mages," I answered as I rose to my feet. Staying put, but now craned my head to glance down the hall behind me. I hated lying, but the only time Autar ever cut out like this was if he was suddenly ill.

Jasmine gave a hum in consideration, but I didn't know if it was about my comment or if she was interested in the lamp again. Her hand hovered over it and the urge to tell her to stop almost blurted out of my mouth as she rubbed the surface.

While she was surprised no magical being was summoned forth offering her everything she desired, I wasn't.

"Strange," she said, and Burhan continued to hold the pillow steady for her. "I'll have to pay a visit to those two and ask what we should do next."

"Of course, Princess. May I be excused?"

She glanced over to me, hands returning to her sides at the oddness of my question. I was meant to take over to Burhan as her standing guard while he took care of the lamp. But I had to know where Autar went.

"You may," she said after a pause. "Here, take this to the armory?"

With a bow, I took the pillow that still held the lamp.

But didn't follow her intended orders as I first went to find Autar. There's no way he could have gone far.

I checked his room, three bathrooms, and all the common areas. And nothing. Frankly, I was about to take the lamp to the armory just because I hadn't checked there for him.

But the mage's rooms were along the way, so I made a detour there. Maybe I hadn't lied. Maybe I drank more than I thought and was half remembering truths.

And for the first time in my life, I was upset that neither of them were here. How does one lose three people? Maybe I'm the one who went mad. Did the cave have worse air than we thought? Was I the only survivor?

No. That didn't make sense. Princess Jasmine mentioned visiting the others still. They had to be here somewhere.

My search continued, searching everywhere in the castle, until the armory was the only place I hadn't looked. It felt like the one place I shouldn't go.

Instead I slumped to the floor outside of it. Holding the lamp in one hand, and a quickly emptying bottle in the other. This time, drinking to remember.

When booze was gone, I pulled the lamp to my chest and closed my eyes tight. "Autar, where are you? *Please…*"

"You don't look so good," he said. "It's okay, I'm here."

I jumped up at the sound of his voice, expecting that holding still caused him to find me first. But the hall was empty. I ran down the hallway, only to collide into someone else equally as large.

"Whoa there," Remmi said. Least he looked the same as usual with the expectation of leaving his apron in the kitchen. "You alright?"

"I... have to deliver this to the armory." Saying anything else would make everyone think I was crazy. *But...* "Have you seen Autar?"

"Let's drop this off together, and I'll make you something to sober you up," Remmi offered, and when I didn't even rise my gaze, he gently turned me around and brought me into the armory.

I placed the lamp down on a new pedestal, and agreed I had to take everything slow. First some food, then water, then I'd figure out what the fuck was going on.

The food didn't sit in my stomach like it usually did after a night of drinking. But I ate it all anyway, took anything offered to me. Remmi cooked, cleaned, and then returned to his wife as I sat in the kitchen slowly working on some bread. I no longer thought I was drunk. Or had even been drunk in the past day. I had definitely gone mad.

"You aren't mad, Hadi," Autar said, across from me. He'd been standing their while Remmi had made me meal. Yet, *I* was the only one who saw him. Meaning he couldn't actually be there.

Guilt must have made me lose my mind.

"I can prove it to you," Autar said, stepping closer as I shuttered back. He frowned before he spoke again. "Just make a wish."

"I wish you'd leave me alone so I could trust my senses

69

again," I mumbled through the mouthful.

And poof. The very solid form of my ex-boyfriend vanished in a puff of smoke.

Chapter Nine

The baker kicked me out before dinner with far less grace than the chef had shown me in this morning. Probably because I had broken into the cabinet that she used to make rum candy.

After being kicked out of my food filled sanctuary, I did my best to avoid everyone. Constantly moving about the castle to duck their rounds.

Only pausing when I found another ghost also acting crazy this morning. If he had what I did, maybe he could fix us.

"Of course I see you," Madison said as he walked back to his room. "With that?" After another few steps he leaned back from the space in front of him. "No need to yell, I'd say you're more translucent right now."

The air in front of him crackled with angry jagged lines of yellow light before flashing out of sight.

"Easy, okay!" His hands lifted up to the invisible storm cloud that was brewing in the room. "Could you please be more specific about what you want?"

Madness had absolutely taken ahold of him too.

"Hadi did what?" The Hatter asked the air, then looked over his shoulder as if knowing where I was.

I stepped back, around the banister so he couldn't see me. *What the fuck is happening?*

Deciding I could hide in my room, I silently pushed off, but the second I turned down the hall Madison was already standing there in my path.

"Eve'n Captain," Madison greeted.

"*Hatter*," I growled back. He lunged at me, and I caught him by the shirt collar. Lifting him away from me and pinning him back against the wall. "What do you want?"

"I need you sober," he said, grinning. "Wasn't expecting the man handling, should I tell you my safe word?"

"Shut the fuck up."

He at least granted me that, and I enjoyed it for all of a second before my stomach started to bubble. Attempting to think nothing of it, until everything under my skin started to fizzle. I dropped the mage, hoping that would be enough to get him to stop.

He landed nimbly on his feet as I had the overwhelming urge to suddenly throw up. Nothing but amber colored booze came up unceremoniously onto the cold tile. *How*—
"Please," I begged, as I wiped my mouth not even sure what I was asking for.

"Why did you wish Autar away?" Madison asked. "Do you not like him anymore?"

"He's gone," I cried out, wishing he hadn't forcefully taken the boozy comfortable distance between me and my fear.

"You are very dumb," Madison declared and grabbed my long hair. Fingers dug into my skull as he somehow overpowered me.

A whimper rattled its way through my rib cage, something in my head snapped, and I collapsed onto the damp floor.

"You really are one dumb fucker," Autar agreed.

Wait... "Autar?" I groaned, holding my head as I pushed myself up to sit back on my heels.

In front of Hatter stood Autar looking different than before. He had been completely solid when I first thought he was haunting me, but now actually looked a bit ghost-like. I could see Madison through him.

No, not a ghost, but a man made of a smoke. There wasn't much definition near his feet, and only gained a solid clarity above the waist.

"You're alive." My heart pounded hard like it wanted to also break free of my stupidity.

"Yeah."

Madison stepped around Autar, chewing on his finger as he inspected his work. "I made him look how he does to me. Think I nailed it, but my vision always a bit jabberwocky."

"You're alive," I repeated, each time sending a crashing wave of relief through myself. "Where are your feet?"

"You saw feet before?" Madison asked.

Autar turned towards Madison, the movement more of a smoke swirl than anything that could be called a step. "I got it from here, thank you."

Madison lifted his top hat off his head in a bow before leaving us. Autar offered his hand to help me up but mine went right through it.

"Guess that doesn't work," Autar sighed, and ended up instead hovering lower. Eye to eye I could almost pretend it was any other day.

"I'm sorry," I blurted. "I'll fix this. I'll make you whole again."

He didn't seem to hear me, or at least didn't acknowledge me. The red tinted smoke losing its color as he moved over to the lamp. That he was able to pick up, and even able to drop it into my hands. "I know you despise magic but, Hadi… I'm jinn now, and you are my master."

"We will go to Jasmine, and we will fix this." I quickly got up to my feet, this time wasted no time in returning to her. Outright even ignoring the guard posted at her throne and storming straight into her courtyard.

Rajah growled at me, before I realized what I had even done. It didn't matter, the lamp was real. We could do anything. Everything. All war gone in a wish.

"By the stars," Jasmine said with a frown. "You don't seem yourself today."

"I know, but look," I said, taking one of her hands and pressing the lamp into it. "It's magic. It grants wishes. Say something, Autar."

"Hello, Princess," he sighed.

The both of us looked in his direction, and I'm certain she can see him too. Until she backed away from me. Confusion and sadness lining her expression. "Maybe I've been too lenient with you."

"Your Highness," I pleaded, looking to Autar for help again before realizing it likely made me look even more mad. "I can wish for peace. For our men to be victorious in battle."

"No, you cannot! Must not," Jasmine said. "If everything you say *is* true, you've captured your fellow guard in a magical prison. If you burn through your wishes, I certainly can't take control only to do the same. It's not justice. Release him."

"I'm actually fine," Autar sighed again. "Not that anyone took a damn second to asked me."

"Return the lamp to the Cave of Wonders," Jasmine ordered.

I glanced down at the lamp in my hands, surely Autar was tied to it. Not like I could just brush my fingerprints off, and have Autar still return home. "Please, just think about it first. Check the laws, and with the strategists, what any member of the guard would want."

Autar rolled his eyes, his smoke curling up and slipping completely into the lamp.

"Give me tonight," Jasmine said, "I'll have an answer for you tomorrow."

Bookshelves stood guarding nothing along the tapestry lined the walls. Within them was a woven version of our history, but I was looking for something older. Knowledge that had been with us before the founding of Wonderland's united kingdoms. My fingers ran over the rough leather bindings checking for the oldest in the castle's collection.

Somewhere between the recorded history and folktale I've found a book on magical creatures, pulled it off the shelf and placed it down on a table for Autar and me to study. Knowledge was the key to any battle. Physical, or otherwise. I carefully flipped though the inked pages until I found a useful passage.

"According to this, jinn are shape shifting spirits made

of fire and air," I raised my gaze off the book to Autar and figured that was mostly what I saw. Fire and air almost sounded like a riddle that would yield smoke.

"It also says jinn can turn plots of land fertile," Autar read aloud. "Certainly don't know how to do that."

"Often unseen, invisible, or abstracts that can speak with humans," I continued reading. "I wonder why you couldn't speak to Jasmine."

"There's this… hum. Almost a song stuck in my head. I think it's what mages can hear within magic. Maybe that's why she couldn't."

"If only mages can see you, why can I?"

"Is that an earnest question, Master?"

Oh no, no, no, no, no.

"We can't—I can't do this 'master' nonsense. Jasmine is right, this is wrong."

"We have, and we are."

Maybe magic made people sound more cryptic. Because I wasn't sure what that meant. "We need… ground rules. To understand how you being like this works."

"Sounds wise."

"Have you," I gestured a hand towards him. "You know, unlocked any hidden knowledge?"

Autar snickered.

"Oh come on, just focus. Try to channel what you are now," I rambled, and continued to flip through the only book we had on jinn in the whole library.

"Ten have possessed the bottle," Autar started, sounding distant enough that I wanted to take his hand. "Ten masters ruled, controlled, dominated."

"Hey, stay with me." I reached for him, and even though it wasn't far enough to touch, the movement caught his eye, and his attention pulls forward along with it.

"What do you want?" Autar asked, "Just to win this war?"

My lips parted realizing that's almost exactly what I overheard from the mages before the battle. And I didn't. At least, not *only*. "I'd just like to understand you now. Know how to…" My words trailed off as I can't bring myself to admit that I want to take care of him.

"I told you, I'm fine. Better than before," Autar said unaware. "Living as human? Now that was the struggle. Always in pain, having to be super strict about what I could and couldn't eat. How hard I pushed my body. This? This is a cakewalk."

"Can you touch other things besides the lamp?"

Autar stared down at the book, hand over the page but when he added any movement the smoke around it dissipated. "Doesn't seem like it, maybe if I could get a better grip on myself."

I laughed, thinking he's making a joke only to realize he's not. Autar looked worried, more lost than I've ever seen him actually. "We will figure this out. I promise."

Burhan cleared his throat as he steps into the room. He can't see Autar either. "Princess Jasmine is ready for you."

We walked into the throne room, and I knew we are in trouble. There's too many people here. A full court means witnesses for an official decree. Jerick, and the other strategists stand on one side. The members of the guard, along with the two mages on the other.

"Agrabah cannot justify magical slavery," Jasmine said, chin held high. "Return the lamp to the Cave of Wonders. Do not bottle the spirit in some other vessel either. Forces such as jinn must not be controlled by one man. They are meant to be free."

I opened my mouth to speak, but I think she recognized that a 'Yes, your Highness' was not about to come and raised her voice to speak over me. "If you do not, you'll be banished for stealing from our most ancient sites. Given your life's work thus far, this is the greatest and only leniency we have to offer."

Jerick glanced down, and I think he had been the one to remind Jasmine that a strict ruling of the law said the penalty was death. They weren't anything ever than fair under the law.

"You'd doom Autar forever to wait in a dark cave for some stranger to stumble along and find him?" I asked, more forceful than I had meant. Autar wasn't gone. At least three of us standing here today could talk to him right now.

I searched out the mages in the crowd. Henri and Madison stood a step apart from the guard, hand in hand, but still on a side that wasn't mine. "Frog Prince, please. Help me."

"I'm sorry," Henri said softly, and to his credit he looked me in the eyes. "I have no power here."

"Does the guard have your compliance, Captain?" Jasmine asked. Voice staining from my newfound defiance already.

Words couldn't be trusted, so I lowered my head and nodded.

"Return the lamp tonight," Princess Jasmine ordered, "I need you back for the rest of this war afterward."

I bowed and started to walk away without saying a thing.

"Hadi!" Autar yelled. His voice vibrated through the lamp in my bag before his smoky form appeared and followed at my heels. "You fucking asshole. After everything, you'd do this to me? Fight!"

My steps didn't slow. Didn't even pause to go rather supplies. I was determined to walk straight into the desert without supplies.

This equally stupid plan on top of the harsh orders engaged Autar as his smoke sizzled like oil on an open fire. Sparks of it flying up as if meant to burn.

But the specks dissolved before they managed to land on my skin. I don't think he could hurt me. How colossally unfair.

"You're…" Autar said softer, realizing something as I looked back to check if we were out of sight from the others. "You're not taking me back?"

"I have to do right by the men in my command," I said, nervously licking my lips. "Human or jinn."

"Oh, thank the stars," he breathed out, drifting further away from my face as if planning to sit down. "Should we tell the mages? They might be sympathetic."

"No, I don't trust them with this. Not with you," I said, clutching the bag a bit tighter to my side.

"Aw."

That tiny syllable wasn't enough to settle my panic, but it didn't matter I had to move forward. No matter what.

"Wait!" Autar yelled.

"Oh my god, what?" I whispered; certain I'd be heard still by anyone around.

"I need you to grab my grandmother's jewelry box from my room."

That little gemmed box was actually the only thing Autar took with him when left the city to come here. It was definitely small enough to slip into my bag along with the lamp, but it was in the opposite direction of where I was headed. "Do you really think now is the time?"

"No one told you to leave this second with nothing but the sword and flask on your belt." The air around Autar rippled. Not quite lightening, but still a bolt of energy I didn't want smite from. "Go get supplies."

"Alright, alright, please just keep the visuals contained."

I knew the schedules by heart having written them and timed my movements to avoid being spotted. Then slipped into Autar's room grabbing the jeweled box. I'd like to fill the rest of my satchel with food, but I don't know the kitchen staff's pattern well enough to risk it.

As I waited to leave the room, a guard passes in front of the door. It would be so easy to just step out and return to my old life. Hell, I could even delegate the lamp's return to any number of guards that weren't at court.

Autar watched over my shoulder, maybe having the same thought. "Are you sure this is what you want?"

Part Two: All That Glitters
Chapter Ten

"You kept me."

It pained me how touched Autar's words sounded. As if I could have ever turned him out into the cold like that. In any context. Ex-boyfriend, or not.

"You kept me," he repeated sounding sad this time. Like an animal whining that they are on a leash. Tied to their owner and dragged through town, instead of running free. "You'll be marked as a deserter. No one can leave the royal guard like that. Not even someone like you. Especially with enemies outside the gates."

"I know the laws!" I yelled, scaring an old woman as she shops the bazaar's colorful fabrics. *Shit.* My hand grabbed onto my cloak's hood pulling it further down over my face. This is the first time since joining the guard that my identity is covered up. Felt poorly done, but no one seems to notice.

"You will be exiled for sure now, because you kept me." This time is a dare. His words somehow hit me like bumping into a brick wall.

"I know, okay. I know. Sorry for getting us into this

mess." Maybe Autar would have been fine if I never touched the lamp again. But I wouldn't be. It's that truth that tore my life part. "I couldn't lose you."

There's silence, so I began walking through town again. Moving towards the only place I know in the kingdom that doesn't have guard patrols to recognize us.

"Thank you," Autar softly added at last.

They weren't ancient, but the crumbling buildings on the outskirts of our city where definitely still ruins. I remember advising Jasmine to leave them alone, pull the guard back from a crime filled area that did not want help despite living amongst the harsh dusty wind.

Maybe it was fitting for me to run to an abandoned guard tower. The bricks long since tumbled from once lofty heights and piled up at the entrance. A ceiling beam that was meant to hold up the door frame had slid out and now blocked it. Slipping over it was a possibility if I could clear it of other debris first.

Three hours later, I had made some progress. There was now a gap where I could look inside at least. Broken sunbeams shined through holes in the roof. The place appeared pretty dilapidated throughout.

Autar appeared at my side with a swirling mist. This time with enough control over his form that his feet attempted to kick broken pottery away to no avail. "Are you going to ask for help?"

"How are you meant to help?" I asked, wiping the sweat from my brow.

"Just say the magic word."

"I am *not* using a wish on this!"

He laughed, his smoky form curling near the bottom in delight. "I meant, please."

My chest puffed out, annoyance growing, and further reminded me of how useless I was for fitting into tight spaces. "Please."

Autar wasn't able to move the bricks directly, so instead he placed a hand near the gap. Wispiness pulling away from him along with the air flow, filling the space with smoke.

The building groaned. Bricks scraped against each other, and I backed up, fast. Rocks piled up at the door shot every which way. Some going in, some out, others hitting the side of the building before coming to rest in a much smaller mound.

"That's—" My jaw dropped, too stunned to form any other words.

Autar's form reshaped on the inside of the tower, eyes raising to catch mine. "I don't think anything can hold me, besides the lamp."

"As the owner of the lamp, you can't do that to me," I said, sweating for a different reason. "Can you?"

"What, hurt you?" Autar asked, I and feared the idea was now in his head. "Probably only if you ask nicely."

My laugh was a purely nervous one, but I don't think he noticed as he attempted to move something else with no luck. With a tsk, he stuck his intangible clenched hand into an already broken banister. When his fingers flicked out, the wood splintered.

"Be careful, will you? If this whole place comes down, I'll be crushed under it." This idea at least gave him pause, and I didn't want to know what exactly he thought and started climbing up the flight of stairs. They were mostly intact, the missing few didn't make much of a difference.

I suddenly stopped when I hit the top of the landing. The openness from the lack of wall making for a stunning beautiful view. The castle sat perfectly in the middle of broken beams like a frame. It looked so grand from here, like someone had painted it better than it was in person.

"Why here?" Autar asked, as if I had a choice.

I turned away from everything that once mattered. "It's called being poor."

"It's called leaving the city. You chose here."

I opted to ignore him, because he wasn't being helpful, and I didn't want to be exploded if I annoyed him in equal measure back.

"Where's that... Robin Hood. Isn't he meant to steal from the rich and give to the poor?"

"Must have never visited these parts," I mumbled, lifting a wooden frame. I think it once was part of a bed. There were thinned out sheets twisted around it. Least someone agreed with my idea of hiding here. "The rest of the guard keeps spreading rumors that he gave up being a hero, and now gets his back blown out by his favorite."

"Is that what you want?"

I turned towards him, gasping as I found him inches from my face. Jinn don't have footfall. No weight to creak the floorboards and let me know he moved closer. This was going to be murder on my sense of personal space. If I could put a bell on him, I would in an instant.

"Whoa, whoa, whoa," I said, holding my hands out low. "I'm good." But I was also curious to the point of being equally guilty of listening to and engaging in the gossip. "Why?"

Autar's eyes narrowed slightly. "Why what?"

Why are you so close? Why did you suggest that? Why do I want to want to shove you away from me as much as I want to pull you closer?

Words felt like loaded charges now. I had to be careful with what I said. There was a limited number of wishes left and in no way could I ever wish on something like that. No matter how horny I get now or in the future. I might be a banished outcast, but I wouldn't be selfish prick.

"Why do you even believe Robin Hood is real?" I asked, before carefully turning back to move the remaining frame and start dusting off what would be passable mat to sleep on.

"You don't believe Merry Men exist?" Autar asked, "It's said they toppled the Queen of Heart's House of Cards. How do you not believe in them? It's… politics."

"Oh, I believe they exist. I think Robin is the fantasy. One that changes based on whatever the rebels need. First a leader, then a symbol of winning and retiring to a happily ever after."

"You're wrong." His tone was harsh and getting angry, or at very least the red hue from the sunset behind him made it look that way. "People like the Mad Hatter exist. The stories we hear from the rest of Wonderland? Those are about real people."

"Whatever you say." I knocked one of the floor pillows against the banister and kicked up a cloud of dust.

"Fine, make your home here."

I *was,* so I went back to ignoring him. This time he seemed aware of it and bottled up his annoyance within the lamp. Where I assume he didn't have to put up with my choices of interior design.

Everything was great, until past dinner time the following day. My stomach growled loudly enough I thought people might think come investigate the strange sounds.

The clouds floating above me started to be shaped like food and I knew my thoughts were be stuck on meals until I found one.

"Made you soup," Autar said.

I had absolutely not wished for that. I'd been dreaming about sinking my teeth into a roast. Since soup was also impossible, I sat up, only to find a bowl sitting on top of intact pottery I turned upside down as a table.

It was possible for a jinn there wasn't much difference between summoning something and delivering something. Or maybe he was just being an ass. Either way, that didn't explain how he got the soup.

After pushing the blankets off myself, I picked up the bowl. Holding it in my hands for a moment as it warmed my fingers. It smelled so divine my stomach rumbled again. "Did you steal someone's dinner?"

"Yes." He crossed his arms, and I decided not to ask any other questions until I at least ate.

I savored every last drop, doing my best to balance out making it last and avoiding it getting cold. "Am I meant to return the bowl?"

The comment was meant as the joke, but Autar rolled his eyes. He worked out how to lean, or at least appeared like he was against the wall overlooking the city. "Is there a gift horse you have not looked in the mouth?"

"I only mean to ask how you are able to selectively move things. Surely someone's dinnerware isn't also magical."

"Haven't figured it out yet," he said, staring out without even a glance towards me. "Been trying to test it all morning. I don't need to eat, but I got this like feeling like I *needed* to bring that, and suddenly I could."

"What is it like out there?"

He shrugged. "Same as we left it. Suppose it is crime filled, or what not. The soup was left out for a cat so don't start about some hypothetical starving family."

I should have told him it was incredible. But I also had to fight back the urge to joke that not even two days back on the street he started stealing. Even if it was from a stray. Instead, I thought of the lamp. "What's it like in there?"

This time Autar had to glance over to see what I was talking about. His eyes grew unfocused, and I started to fear the answer.

"I feel small, but not cramped. It's like floating in a black sea, but without fear of waves crashing over you. No sense of time. It's the darkest, quietest thing I've ever experienced."

"Sounds lonely."

His eyes flicked up to mine, then gestured around to the room. "Better than this."

Chapter Eleven

Without food, booze, or anyone searching for us I figured it was time to scout the area for myself. Learn what's around, who's in charge, and how I could quietly exist in the background.

The streets felt tight compared to the rundown airy guard tower. Handmade mashrabiya screens covered the windows above. Their patchwork of mismatched designs cast uneven and ever-changing patterns on the ground as we walked through. The seasoned smells of family dinners hidden behind the privacy screens made me feel like an intruder. There was minimal foot traffic here compared to the other markets in town and the type of wares being offered reflected that. Larges pieces of discarded wood could easily be slid over each shop's entrance, so the merchant didn't have to worry with selling out every day.

"Hey, don't I know you?" a young voice called. A figure was hidden in the shadows, and I took a step under the makeshift room allowing my eyes to adjust.

Sitting at a counter, chewing slowly on a piece of grizzle was a teenage boy. His tunic's sleeves were cut off as if to show the muscles he still needed years to fully bulk up.

"You're that fucking guard."

The memory of grabbing him by the shirt scruff and pulling him back away from Jasmine's castle seasons ago come back to me. "What of it, kid?"

He scoffed, then spit out what he'd been chewing on. "Nothing, old man."

"Is that Jafar's son?" Autar leaned in over my shoulder. "Was his family exiled, or hiding here too?"

I nodded to answer to the first part, and hoped it looked like I just accepted my age. As for the second question, I actually didn't know. Jafar had been kicked out of the court for manipulating Jasmine's farther. The man himself never seen from again, but his family was still within the city.

"What are you doing here?" I asked hoping the answer could be applied to Autar's questions as well.

"What it look like?" the boy answered.

Honestly? It looked like he was bored. Age wise he was old enough to stop finding much enjoyment in running around all way. Teenagers needed a school interest, or friends their own age to speak with.

This was a shop, and I was the only one that could be considered a customer. And he definitely wasn't trying to get my coin in exchange for excellent service. "Did you go into business for yourself?"

"Business is a rich man's game."

"Clever kid," Autar commented, and he floated further inside the shop. There was no pattern to what was stocked. It looked like items from a junkyard that been cleaned to the best of one's ability. Autar's hand lifted towards a lantern that had the glass sides knocked out of its frame. In replacement hung colorful tissue paper. When Autar touched the metal, the wind gently blew through.

The movement caught both our attention, while Autar's expression lit up with delight. "I'm getting better at this."

I gritted my teeth, looking to the boy again who was not letting this new curiosity fade away. "At making the place haunted," I mumbled under my breath.

"What?" The boy asked, then rolled his eyes. "Look, you buying something or are you here to harass me again?"

I very much had never harassed him in my life, unless telling him no and doing my job counted.

"It's fine, Hadi," Autar said, sounding equally annoyed if not more. "It's just an object that easily moves. See?" He started waving his hands through the rest of the packed store and his arm disappeared motionlessly into the mix.

The display was actually a little funny so I looked away so I wouldn't end up smiling at what appeared to be nothing. "What's your name, kid?"

"Nonya."

"Really?"

The teenager laughed, while Autar was the one to shake his head this time. "Stars, you are old. As in 'none of your business'."

"Ah. We'll be going then."

Nonya made a show to look around at only the seemingly two of us. "Did the guard fire you for going crazy?"

"Yeah, something like that." I stepped out of the store, Autar silently followed behind me, but only after he hit at the paper lantern again like an annoyed cat.

I always told myself that I saved Autar from the life of crime. Got him off the streets and gave everyone in the guard a better life. And maybe it was better for those suffering, longing for change. But mostly? It was just different.

To me, the royal guard, and the tree we wore over our chest represented our shared roots, shared family, shared future. To those under Jafar's lineage, it bore nothing but poisoned fruit. The truth of the matter *didn't* matter. Who had been in the wrong, seemingly predestined by whatever side someone had been already born into.

No one else called out to me as we silently just watched life move around us. Stealing was natural here. Akin to how an animal eating another in the wild was simply the circle of life. If anyone got too prideful, thought themselves the king of this hill, the guard has, and would again, come. Sort out who was the rightful owners of the goods in question. They wouldn't change why things had been stolen in the first place. That task was beyond the guard.

The thefts weren't seemingly personal, but the exchanges were. A basket of apples for a beaded set of earrings. A hairbrush for knitted blanket. Currency was kept only to interact with the other parts of town. If you had none of either, you took what you wanted. And I was not an exception to that. Instead of a loaf of bread, when given the opportunity, I grabbed booze. Simply because the alcohol made me happier than breakfast could.

By late afternoon, I wasn't even the only drunk just hanging out on the street with anyone else who didn't want to be in their homes. Kids were laughing, shouting, running around, and ignoring the warnings of their parents.

Least the ones that had adults watching over them. There were definitely a handful that must have escaped the orphanage or never been. You could see it in their faces. Not from dirt, but the hard gaze in their eyes.

If there was a leader among them, it would have been Nonya. He stood with a foot against a wall watching them all. "Omar!" He shouted to younger boy who had just pushed the girl he was playing with down on the ground.

Omar glanced back to Nonya, then grabbed the ball she had. All too casually Omar took the toy, and other kids hollered their excitement as he brought it over for them.

I walked over to girl, who had pulled her legs up close, and now watched the others play without her. "Hey, kid. I'm Hadi, what's your name?"

"Ruthie," she mumbled as she glanced up at me, then her eyes shifted to where Autar was standing. "Who's he?"

"Me?" Autar said in surprise, looking to me before back at the girl who clearly could see him. "Are you a mage?"

"I'm no one," Ruthie said, resting her head on her knees.

"Nonsense." I pulled my short sword off my belt, and she pressed herself further up against the wall. If I had still been a captain, I could have offered enlisting her. Given actual protection. *Now what did I have?* "Here."

She stared at the sword I held out in disbelief before her hand slowly reached up to take it from me.

"Do you know how to use it?" Autar asked.

"A weapon is a weapon," Ruthie replied, knowing either far too much or far too little about such things.

I attempted a smile. "Remember one thing for me?" When she nodded, I continued. "This isn't to protect your property. It's to safeguard what's really important."

"You aren't no one, Ruthie," Autar said, "*You* are what matters."

She smiled up at Autar and it warmed my heart. Least until her gaze shifted behind him and her expression fell. "I have to go," she said, and scampered up.

I watched her run down the street, before finally turning

to see what she had been afraid of.

"There's something different about you," Nonya said, eyes not pulling away from me. He clearly only saw one of us. "Once I figure out why you are behaving this way, I'm going to take whatever caused this difference in you."

I lifted my chin to look down at him. A bully like his father had been. "And why would you do that? A grudge for not being allowed into the castle years ago?"

Nonya shook his head. "Because if there's something that can change someone as by the rules as you, then it could change anything." He studied me from head to toe not seeing anything of interest, before swiping at my bag.

I turned, causing him to collide into my broad side. "You don't know what you are talking about." We backed off as he shook off the dazed feeling. I'm not going to let anyone, let alone some punk ass kid, take the lamp from us. Thankfully, he's doesn't follow us down the street.

"We wouldn't be in this situation if it wasn't for the damn Hatter's nonsense," I grumbled under my breath. "If we still had Jasmine's ear, we could convince her that people in this area need help."

Autar's not listening to me, focused instead up on Ruthie even further down the way. She's swinging the sword around, out of the way of everyone and I'm not sure what the issue is since she's clearly a natural.

"Would you at least listen to me when I'm talking to you?" I scoffed. "I look crazy enough when overheard, so you could at least acknowledge me."

"I'm sorry, I'm listening," he sighed, and I knew he wasn't done yet. "It's just... back in the guard it never fixed... *everything*. Your homesickness is doing the talking."

"What? If it was so bad, then why did you stay? There's no conscription."

"It didn't say it was *so* bad either," Autar said, getting defensive about the wording.

"You still didn't answer my question."

His jaw set, fighting back answering before he gave in. "All I know for sure is you are a bigger ass than ever."

The whole next morning, I compared everyone's movements to what they had been before. Seeing their natural patterns, and the gaps between where no one was paying attention. My thievery was really getting out of control. Beyond taking what was needed to survive.

My concentration was on a worn-in deck of cards. We used to issue a deck to each member of the guard. It was such a casually available thing I hadn't thought about bringing any with us. Would be good for one player or many. Autar and I could even play together if I dealt.

"Just take it," he said, over my shoulder. I almost expected him to float over to my other side to talk some sense into me. Be reasonable. *Be good.* Instead… "No one is watching, Hadi."

He was fixed at my side, driving my head crazy over the fact I couldn't smell his sweat or feel his breath. If I had wanted to pull him closer, I'd come up short. It all gave my loneliness a bitter taste.

"You could run this whole block if you wanted," Autar continued as I refused to take my eyes off the cards even as the people playing left to so grab their food. "Just how benevolent can one convict be?"

I stepped away from Autar and walked straight up to the

table. Gathered the cards and moved away without a single pause in my step. The deck was dropped into my bag as I made for the tower.

When you fight alongside people, you assume their morals are yours. Within an army, there's guidelines everyone follows. Autar's still following, but a glance towards him shows he's smirking over the fall out of his suggestion.

With a heavy heart, I realize the one that put a moral compass into his hand was me. His true north of right and wrong isn't known at all.

"Deuces Wild?" Autar asked, looking like the soldier I knew. Even with the single deck there's now an infinite collection of possibilities that could grant us a smidge of joy, and I find myself unable to feel all that guilty.

Crime did made my life better. "How do I let you convince me to do these things?"

"Just clever like that, I guess."

No, that wasn't it at all. None of this had to do anything with being stronger or outwitting someone else.

"What is it?"

I shook my head, wondering if I was ready for the weight of these realizations.

Chapter Twelve

"I believe in the rule of threes. We used one wish already; we are not wasting another one."

"*You* wasted the first one." Autar's voice boomed and he might have even gotten a mite larger along with it. "I have a different set of needs now as a jinn. And I'm begging you to make another wish. I don't care how stupid you make it."

Mean and pushy is a new look on Autar. Maybe even literally since he looked more like a wispy ghost, as if at risk of being blown away on the wind then the solid bear of a man I've known for years. I'm not even sure if I can trust him right now. His appearance does worry me though. If Autar doesn't need to eat or breathe anymore. What were his needs?

"I need to serve you," Autar pleaded, softer this time. "Before I lose my mind, *please.*"

Being the drunk self-hating asshole that I am, I say the very first thing that comes to my mind when pushed. "I wish you'd go fuck yourself."

Autar's form tinted pink. The blush wasn't just over his cheeks, but his flameless smoke gained the hue throughout.

"I'm going to make you regret that wish."

"Uh huh." I tipped the bottle to my lips, and found it empty of booze. Even shake it upside down to double check before tossing it. "Already do." The glass smashed, and my eyes follow the sound before I look back towards Autar and find he's not there.

Which is fine for now because the drinking is making my head full of lustful things that I don't want to share with anyone. Having him around would more encourage the stray thoughts.

"Thank the stars, you're back!" In an instant, I stood up to greet the jinn that floated back into the highest level of the tower, never needing a single stair.

Autar looked better, so clearly the time part has helped him. *I probably did a good by telling him to take a break from me.* He'd been away long enough that I thought finding the Hatter to mess with my head might be needed again.

"I'm here to fulfill your wish," Autar said, voice laced with heat.

Wait, what had I wished for? *Oh no.* "I—I didn't mean anything by it. Therefore I shouldn't count, right?"

"You did, and it does." There's no wiggle room in his tone, just firm, judge-free, and definite. His clothes start coming off. If this is a habit or strip tease, I'm not sure which since Autar can change shape by thinking it.

"There's no use pretending you don't still desire me," he said, "I can feel it. Which is why I'm going to do the one thing you can't do to me."

Lords, I was in trouble. I swallowed roughly, my eyes already dropping to gaze over his muscular chest. This wasn't fair, it's not like he even needed to be so fit anymore. "What's that?"

"Touch me." His hands shimmied out of his pants, and I'm staring at his firm ass as he moved to lounge on the thin mats where I usually sleep.

No, no, no. I can't watch this. My eyes snapped shut and silently vowed not to look.

Autar made an amused sound before his breath hitched, and I was left to imagine what he was doing to himself. Which only made this situation feel all the naughtier.

"You can watch."

His words were pure torture. I shouldn't want this, but my mind and body still desperately did. My hand reached towards my own pants just to adjust myself.

"Nuh uh," Autar said softly, "The audience does not get to participate."

My mouth went dry. Would wishing for water interrupt and stop this or would he find a way to drown me with that desire too?

I took a peek as his hand moved up and down his considerable length. As I stood there, obscenely watching as the only serious boyfriend I've ever had jerk himself off because I had been crass towards his needs. My failure within these facts only made the situation more conflicting.

The worst part was that he wasn't even pleasuring himself crudely, as if in revenge. To say, 'fuck you, this is what you lost'. No, that would have been justice.

This? As he made a literal show out of the way his muscles flexed, head lulled, hand moved rhythmically to a beat my body yearned to follow. This was outright my very own, very weird, pornographic dream.

When Autar came, I was the one who shivered the most. He sighed deeply, body relaxing with a blissful heavy haze. "I needed that," he said, with a slight laugh. "Almost feel like a real boy again."

I knew that was meant as a joke, but I couldn't find the humor over my own guilt. Why had I been so mean to him? Couldn't I have showered him with affection? Admitted that I was sorry for getting us into this whole mess.

He must hate me. Probably did this out of spite over the fact that I clearly wasn't over him. Not completely. Likely less than I had even realized.

"What did," I started to say, knowing my mouth was getting the better of my sense again, "you think about?"

"Your wish, stupid." Autar smirked, as he stretched out on the mat. "I just took advantage of the situation for my benefit."

My lips parted to go on, but he fell asleep before I could reply. Chest gently raising and falling with a content spent look on his face. He figured out sleeping again? I wasn't sure what was happening, but rest was always good.

Of course, he was also still naked. In the middle of a squatted literal hole in the wall that we kept pretending was a proper place to stay. This wouldn't do any longer.

I grabbed the blanket off to the side, and reflexively laid it across him. Already scolding myself for forgetting he was intangible nearly every time anything interacted with him now. But this time? The blanket did not fall through. It perfectly traced his outline of his body.

He hadn't said I wasn't allowed to touch *after*. I reached out; afraid it was all a trick of light, and my hand would phrase through him startling us both. But it didn't. I could feel his arm through the blanket. My heart raced; *this* was what I wanted. I'd been too angry to admit it. It hadn't *needed* to be sexual. I just wanted to feel as if he was really with me.

I fell back, sitting on the floor, and watched him sleep. Magic never made sense, and Autar's had an even greater strangeness to it. But I still could promise myself things. Impossible things, like I always had, and often failed. But still could task myself with taking care of the men alongside me. And never let Autar suffer for my failures again.

Chapter Thirteen

When Autar woke up, he too appeared confused that there was a blanket over him. All his clothes had magically returned without the need to dress, and started to tug up the blanket over his legs. "Did you put this over me?"

"Yes." The admission made me feel somehow equally embarrassed as watching him pleasure himself. An ex could lust over the other, *or* emotionally still care. Both verged back into our relationship territory. "Uh, and I also split up the space better, so you didn't have to go... wherever you go when you leave. Unless you still wanted to, that is."

Autar blinked at the worldly possessions that he made me grab when we fled, things that had been stuffed away and willfully ignored until now. "Wow, thank you."

His hand clutched the blanket for a moment, before pulling it around him like he was still nude. He smiled over at the lamp and a jewelry box that were now sitting proudly under a sunbeam.

It wasn't enough, but it was hope.

"The blanket is different," Autar said, after he folded it up. It looked like his fingers were trying to pick a string off the fabric, but I didn't see any strays. "I can't seem to…"

"Can't seem to what?" I asked softly, he blinked up at me. Almost baffled as I walked over to look along with him.

"Nothing, it's stupid."

"No, tell me." I encouraged, before leaning in to try to see whatever he'd clearly seen. "How is it different?"

Autar stared at me for a long moment, before licking his lips and turned his attention down to the blanket again. "There's gold woven in the fabric. Just this one thread, so I thought it had been picked up from elsewhere. It's invisible to you?"

After squinting, shifting my weight, and stepping over to the other side of him, I still couldn't spot anything that he could be talking about. "Can't see it, sorry."

"I think objects must get these, sometimes. Like that lantern that kid fixed. But I don't understand magic enough to know what it means."

"Means you stole my blanket from me," I teased slightly.

He caught my gaze and smiled. "You never let me do that back in camp."

As a group, all the guards were issued the same blankets. They'd never been a reason to swap it with another's. Logical or not, the comment made me chuckle. "Guess you're right, we aren't home anymore."

He sighed and stepped forward placing the folded-up blanket next to the lamp. Then took a moment to appreciate the jewelry box he'd always kept with his things. Maybe

Autar's home wasn't ever a place, just the memories he brought along for the journey.

"Hey, I don't remember you grabbing this. Is it yours?" Autar asked, lifting the chain of a pocket watch out.

"Absolutely not my style, and how are you touching that so easy?" I blinked, trying not to wonder in too much detail to what else he could touch now.

"Because this is clearly fully magic." He whistled before looping the silver chain over his hand and sat the watch in the center of his palm. Autar admired the face a moment before lifting it to his ear. "I think it belongs to the Mad Hatter."

I groaned. "Not you question you, but…"

"You're fine," he mumbled, still listening to something. "It sings. Tells the date?" Autar moved his hand back in front of him to look at again, and the edges started to melt.

In an instant, Autar pulled away and the watch fell to the ground. Chain trailing after it like a fishing line. I stepped over to check if it was broken.

"Careful," Autar warned, the second I started to bend down. "I think it's made of mercury."

I was determined not to tell Autar he was wrong ever again. But I've never seen mercury in solid form. It had a ridiculously low melting point. Our desert never reached that level of cold. The watch was solid looking on the ground, in the silence between our words I could hear it ticking. "It must behave differently for mages."

Carefully, chain first, I picked up the watch. No music, no date, and no more melting. What a strange oddity. If the Hatter had given it to Autar… why?

"Hadi," Autar breathed out in a whisper.

"Hmm?" I asked, not glancing up until he started

swaying. My hand instinctually reached for him but left me with goosebumps as I caught nothing but air.

He carefully lowered himself to a sit down, or at least a facsimile of sitting. I was worried he'd start coughing and actually fall through the floor. "My hand is all pins and needles."

I desperately wanted to hold his other hand, give it a reassuring squeeze. While I absolutely did not trust the Mad Hatter, there was no way he'd willingly or randomly hurt Autar. If it had been for me, why hide it in Autar's personal stuff that had been in his room back at the castle?

No, there was something else happening here. I placed the watch down as far away as possible in our space, then sat along the same wall next to him. "I'm here, okay? I won't go anywhere unless you ask me to."

"You're making me feel like I'm back in the infirmary," Autar said, looking far too tired to speak.

"No," I sighed. Shame lodging in my chest. If we were the infirmary had healers who might have been able to help. They often hadn't been able to when he was flesh and blood, and if they hadn't again, least the mages would have been closer with the answers over what was happening. There was nothing to do but wait until the mercury exposure waned. "You're here with just me."

"All the better." A ghost of a smile appeared on his face. "Can you... scoot?"

Without really being sure what he meant, I moved forward a bit, and he gave me a weak thumbs up before his hand tremored.

"Can see you better now. I'll be okay," he mumbled. Autar stared ahead, less falling asleep than he appeared drugged.

Maybe I would pound that Hatter into tiny pieces. But

Autar needed me first. I stood up, grabbed the blanket, and placed it over his legs. It once again, sat there in a frozen soft wave over the curves of his body.

As long as it did that, I could convince myself that this was any other night where I stayed up with him. If anything, maybe this was still progress. It was better than yesterday.

We don't really move or speak for an hour or so. It's enough that he's looking a bit better, or at least looked less pale under indirect sunlight.

"Can I see it again?" Autar asked softly.

"The watch?"

He nodded.

I was honestly surprised I hadn't hurled it out of the window. "Let me hold it, okay?"

He paused, then nodded again.

I got up and brought it over. It looked like such an innocently simple thing sitting in the palm of my hand.

"It has strings too," Autar said softly. His hand hovered as if considering plucking one before deciding against it. "Maybe it's still attached to the Mad Hatter. If I need to find him or something. Good thing I have you to hold on to it for me."

I swallowed roughly and avoided his eyes as he stood up. Autar shook out the blanket out in front of him. When his hand moved close to me, I jerked back. "What are you doing?"

"Hold still," he said, eyes focused on something between us. His finger plucked the air before he laughed to himself. "They sound like music."

We might still have a problem. "You do realize you sound crazy, right?"

"I do," Autar smiled.

If he was out of his mind, he didn't seem very alarmed by it. Which is probably why my follow up question was as stupid and petty as I was capable of. "Does the string to me look like the Hatter's?"

Autar shook his head, glancing back to the watch for a moment. "There's a lot on the watch. I can see them all now. It's like my eyes weren't adjusted to all of the colors before. The one from you to the blanket is just a single gold thread."

"This is very weird."

All within the next second, I thought I had something offensive and wanted to back up and say anything else, but Autar just nodded. "Yeah."

"Do you want to get out of here?" I asked, it's not like he literally needed fresh air but maybe somewhere nicer together would still be... nice.

Autar grinned, looking cruelly irresistible again. "Lead the way."

Chapter Fourteen

We sat outside a bakery. It wasn't anything really more than a tight one room kitchen with a counter splitting up the space and a mismatched table and chairs outside. Here money wasn't a problem because yesterday's stale bread was set aside free for anyone.

This time, I was glad Autar didn't eat, because taking double for us both felt like a line too far. I chewed the tough bread and was perfectly content to just sit and enjoy the smell of lemon and cinnamon.

Occasionally Autar would comment on something, and I'd reply, causing anyone leaving with warm bread to awkwardly glance in my direction. It should have bothered me more, but I enjoyed my company.

Kids played out of sight, their yelling voices carrying loudly. Their screams to each other are nothing out of place until something shifts and the adults, who were casually ignoring them before, start running in their direction.

Autar and I get up to follow, hoping if someone is in trouble we can lend a hand. As we come across where the kids had been planning, I realize with a sinking feeling that I may have caused this.

Ruthie is standing away from everyone else, sword out as if ready to wield it. *Again.* "That's what he gets for harassing me after I told him to stop!"

Her justification is ignored as the surrounding adults are trying to see if there's anything that can be done for Omar's stab wound. When there doesn't seem to be, one adult stands. Towering over Ruthie as she holds her sword tighter.

Nonya is the one who stepped in between them. "Back off. Omar was part of my crew. That means this is mine to deal with it."

It takes his veiled threat and the sobbing of the parents to make a witness to it all back-off. I've seen death plenty, but kids getting hurt is always worse. An adult has the understanding and independence to make choices fully for themselves.

The tragedy makes it even easy to just take whatever. I'm no longer even subtle about it. Grabbing bottles, one for each hand, and sampling each without consideration for their owners as I deem them good enough to keep. And no one dares to stop the strong-armed brute who gave out the weapon in the first place.

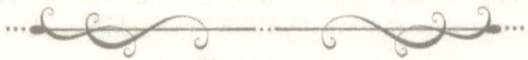

I stumbled into my place and probably would have toppled straight back out into the street below if my magical force of an ex-boyfriend didn't block the gaping hole in the landing's wall. The stairs were hard, and I wanted to crumble onto the floor.

"You're meant to be my keeper," Autar chastised, and I stayed standing out of spite. "Please get it together."

"Why do you get to say please," I slurred, "and don't have desires that get magically filled?"

Autar's expression might kill me if the alcohol doesn't beat him to it.

"I wis—"

"Don't you fucking dare!" Autar pressed a hand to my mouth.

He's not exactly corporeal, so the finger that shushed me not only moved through my lips but past my teeth and over my tongue.

"You wasted two wishes already with stupid drunken remarks, and I will not be humiliated again with the last one. Think before you speak in my presence."

Damn, I didn't know Autar could be so commanding. It's sexy. He'd only ever been able to prove himself while taking orders before. Never giving them. It was as sobering as a bucket of water to my face.

My mind perversely mixed this version of him with the thought of drunkenly messing around back when we liked each other. Made my ability to speak clearly even further out of my capabilities right now. Instead, just nodded like a good little soldier. After a moment, I remembered how to get my mouth to work again. "Would it help to know that was the hottest thing you've ever said to me?"

"Not right now!"

"Yes, sir," I said, with a nod. "Sorry, sir."

Autar grunted, and I'm not sure if he loved my reply or loathed it. "Good," he said, eyes narrowed suspiciously. "Now, sit down so I can pull off your shoes."

I sat. Wobbled a bit on the seat, but thankfully it's low enough that my hand could reach the floor and right myself. "You can't directly inter— interf— touch me."

"I think I can right now," he breathed. And lo-and-behold, his hands lifted my foot off the ground. Autar still felt cold through the boot, but he can move through the world as if human again.

"How is this possible?"

The words are so soft I'm not even sure Autar heard until his expression grew thoughtful. "I think it's because you need it. Please just accept the help and don't ruin this."

"I don't need help."

Autar frowned, and it was another thing I hated myself for. "You're shaking."

I lifted my hand to test his words, to prove he's just making me cold, but my fingers wobble on their own. Huh, I was shaking.

Involuntarily, my eyes find Autar again. Now finding words far too easy to say all of a sudden. "I'm sorry, I'm a mess. I don't understand how you ever put up with me."

"Hush, habib. I got you," Autar said, soothing my fears. He took the other shoe off and stepped back to gather a clean cloth and canteen. It strung when pressed to my brow. I don't even remember what cut me. Actually, no, it had been someone's bottle during the bar fight. I didn't deserve this care.

"Yes, you do," Autar whispered as he continued to clean my face.

I hadn't said anything. I know I didn't that time. And yet he heard me. *Stars, he's so kissable this close.*

Autar either doesn't hear that thought or has the good sense to resist on both our behalf. He stroked my hair, before standing to return the supplies to the tiny pile. And for just that second, I felt like this awful place might be a home someday.

Being drunk was something I was used to. Having a hangover, and powering through because I had a mission and people to look out for was what I was good at. Without that ritual in my life, there hadn't even been a reason to stop drinking. And I realized at the worst possible time that I lacked the ability to exist without booze.

I woke up with the shakes under Autar's watchful eye. Felt again like the worst person for having him trapped in an itty-bitty living space or a broken-down building and I vowed to myself never to drink again.

And over the next couple of days, I had completely convinced myself again that he was a hallucination that was only upgraded to ghost since his touch was freezing anytime it stopped me from going anywhere.

I probably would have broken my self-made promise and found myself another drink if I thought I had the ability to safely walk down the flight of broken stairs. Sitting still felt difficult enough. Anything more made me dizzy.

By the third day, I was throwing up anything I was offered. Not that I accepted much in the first place, given how nauseous I was. I blamed my sweat on the heat, and it was excessive to the point I just let myself cry, with the thought that the tears wouldn't be noticed.

They were, of course. Autar continued to soothe me, reminding me I was still fairly young and hadn't put in a lifetime of drinking yet. That I'd be okay if I could just suffer through it all a little longer. His care felt so damn mean somehow right now. I could go back to my old self if I just had one more drink.

111

What would things have been like if I hadn't taken that lamp in the first place? I'd probably still be a functional alcoholic with an endless supply of bottled sprites and motivation.

By the fifth day, I wondered how I survived without medical help. The setting sun turned the sky the most beautiful shades I've ever seen. Autar watched it with me. Looking stoic and almost whole. Like helping me, helped him. I couldn't stand it and suddenly wanted booze again.

Autar pushed himself off the wall he was leaning against. Coming closer, as if to block my path. "I need something from you."

"Okay." My heart beat fast, and I told myself it was because I still had feelings for him, instead of another withdrawal symptom. "Name it."

"Make a wish that you will never drink alcohol again."

"What? No." I laughed at the very idea. "Don't be silly, I'm not wasting our last wish ever on that."

"If they are *our* wishes," Autar said poignantly, "then it's my turn to make one. I want this. It broke my heart seeing you like that; I don't want to do it again. Next time could easily be worse."

"That's my problem, I'll take care of it." I moved away, and Autar reached for me. Hand coming up with nothing but air again. The coldness still stopped me, and then I had a curious thought. What if the lamp's magic wasn't trying to curse me? What if it was trying to guide me to where I was meant to be?

I turned back to Autar, his expression pained, and in that moment really did want to make him any promise he wanted. "Okay, you're right. I'm sorry for my stubbornness."

"Wish it."

His words sounded near prayer, and I held my hand out as if with enough focus I could need him enough again to be able to touch. His hand mirrored mine as our fingers very nearly did just that. "Wish I would," I started, licking my lips, "never drink again."

Autar's chest hitched with relief and his fingertips felt almost warm under mine. It was the least showy, but most magical moment I could ever ask for. To be cared for this much, by anyone, let alone someone I promised to protect but repeatedly hurt. This level of loyalty could never be earned, it has to be gifted, and carefully respected.

Chapter Fifteen

The next day, I was not my best self. I had fully and completely wanted to keep the promise I made to Autar. I thought because I had wished it would magically become easy. *Poof.* Not an alcoholic.

But my head was screaming at me, and I'd have done anything for another drop.

"Where are you going?" Autar asked.

"Shut up." That's all I said, even as he added more. I really couldn't afford to have this conversation and I didn't need the added witness to my willpower's failure.

Everything from before is gone, so I ventured through the market looking for more. A merchant nodded a greeting towards me that I return and looked over his offerings. Without ability to pay, I just slowly pretend to look for my favorite until he got bored and looked away.

When I lifted a bottle, it shimmered a golden color. A jolt of surprise caused it roll out .of my hand. I expect the glass to crash against the ground alerting its rightful owner. The sloshing bottle made nothing more than a dull thump. The shopkeeper glanced back at me, equally confused by my empty handled surprise.

Unable to believe I'm doing magic; I gave up on all pretense and headed toward those drinking outside. Grabbing cups out of the hands of strangers and watched as it too turned gold.

Autar glimmers each time this happens, and his bitter amusement has worked its up way into a giggle over my antics.

There were plenty of people in this bar, and I planned to try every last drop until one worked. But all of it turned into liquid gold. People are more stunned at the precious metal than upset over losing their alcohol.

"Hadi, stop. It tickles," Autar begged, laughing so hard that he wiped tears from his eyes.

This distracted me long enough that I didn't drop a wine bottle and push on to another. The bottle's weight only grows in my hand. Solidifying further and he shivered as the wine turned solid. "*Uh...* kay, do what you want. This feels great."

I glared at him, probably looking extra mad to those who can't see the jinn among them. "Are you getting off on this?"

"If sex felt like this..." Autar started, chin tilting up as if to savor the lingering feeling as I stopped stealing people's drinks. "I'd never stop."

I growled, grabbing one more bottle on my way out. It turned solid before I even make it a step past the door. Doesn't even give me the satisfaction of breaking into pieces when I hurl it. *"Well?"*

Autar rolled his shoulders, standing there as if he's the one waiting on me. "Well, what?"

"Explain," I demanded, but Autar didn't answer. We

start a loop that ends of with 'explain what'. I groaned before trying again. "What the fuck is happening to you?"

"It's the wish. Every time you try to drink, magic pulls up through me. Feels like I have a body that actually works and exists to do what I want. Also, this is the funniest thing to ever happen to me. I could take on God right now. I've never felt so pain-free."

"I'm about to show you some, fucker."

Autar is still greatly amused as I grabbed for him. He's easily able to move away at first, before his laughter becomes a determinant as my entire focus became wanting to wring his neck.

As my fingers caught him, he gasped sharply. Afraid I might turn Autar into gold, I quickly back off. He shivered and I'm afraid my touch is like the watch's mercury, and able to make him sick.

"Whoa," he said, and with a shake glitter falls off of him. "That felt fucking strange."

"Where's your mage, flatfoot?" Nonya yelled through the crowd, shoving his way through. "You can't deny having one now."

Shit.

"I know where we need to go," Autar said, and moved unnaturally fast ahead of me that I have to sprint to even catch him. "Someone who will help us."

Without time to ask where and who, I just follow. I don't know why he brought us back to the tower and moved up the stairs as if to show me the exact path. Then paused only at the pocket watch.

"No, not them," I beg him. "Please, Autar."

"Pick it up."

My head hangs for a moment before I do as ordered. Autar only gives me a second until he winds back down the stairs, showing me where I'm to go next.

Chapter Sixteen

I'm out of stamina by the time we make it across town. Autar gives me zero time to catch my breath and demands I keep up my top speed the whole way there. If I lag too far behind his eyes lose focus on the string of magic that will take us to the Mad Hatter and he demands I pick up the pace.

I don't even think we are in the right place because this is within city limits and away from the castle. The housing community here is largely for war veterans who retired or have been widowed.

If it's the second, I especially don't want to come begging for help over the mess I made.

"We are sorry to disturb you," Autar called from outside the door of the small residence. This whole home is likely smaller than the rooms they were given in the castle.

I don't think they are here, but I knocked all the same to try to help Autar before glancing around to see if we've garnered any unwanted attention.

"Hadi and I have no one else to ask. We need help understanding this magic between us. We... we keep turning things into gold."

The door suddenly swung open, and we both took a step back. "You did what?" Madison asked, flustered, and looking deeply bewildered. His attention is alarmingly very focused on the both of us.

"We made gold?" Autar repeated and looked towards me for help to explain.

"When I touch alcohol, bottles, cups, anything with it inside. They turn to gold so I can't drink it." I scratched my head, not really wanting to discuss the whole how of this.

Madison moved out of sight, only to return with a wine glass. The speed of which he shoved it towards me made some spill.

His motion abruptly stopped, making more slosh out. For a moment, I think he's debating the ethics of giving an alcoholic booze before he changed his hold on the glass and pushed it towards me again.

I barely caught the stem of the glass out of reflex as he ripped his hand back away. The deep red wine first froze over before a shimmering wave traveled around the glass and within a moment the whole thing was solid gold.

"Henri, come here quick!" the necromancer yelled, with wide eyes that didn't leave me. "And bring your drink!"

My gut tightened over what might happen next that might explain why they are living here now. If that Frog Prince is a walking corpse, or like a pet rock, I'm just going to let the mob take me.

I tried to hand Madison's drink back, but he quickly backed away from me.

"What are we celebrating?" Henri asked as he stepped into view. "Oh, hello. Why didn't you invite them in?"

The former prince looks absolutely the same as we left

him. If anything, Henri seemed in a better mood. Relaxed as if on permanent vacation.

"Hadi is turning things into gold," Autar said, although I'm not sure how that's the answer to what Henri asked.

Henri looked less afraid, but equally curious over this bit of news. "May I see?" He's at least willing to take the glass from me, as Madison flitted around Henri to his other side.

"Alchemy from a non-magical thing is… is wrong," Madison whispered.

I groaned. He was annoying before I was cursed with this cruel joke that prevented me from drinking. "It's clearly Autar's doing."

Madison smiled over at Autar. "You listened to my watch."

Remembering that hunk of magical metal was also in my hand, I offered it to him. To my surprise, he was willing to take the pocket watch back.

"This shouldn't be possible." Henri was focused to the point of ignoring me, and I can't pinpoint why they are surprised. It's happened to Autar and me plenty already today. If it was just some magical fluke it wouldn't happen so consistently.

"No one can create more gold. It's why it's so precious. Transmutation is wickedly strong magic, and even it cannot create something as aged as gold," Henri explained.

Madison moved closer to size up Autar, but he was also being very careful to not touch near the slight translucent blur around the jinn's edges. "It's usually very costly as well."

Autar smiled weakly back, before a wine bottle got shoved into his hands, then repeated with me. Nothing happened as Autar held it, as I tried to explain to them originally. *I'm the cursed drunk.*

"Come inside," Henri said, and moved over to the living room couch. "How did this all start? What wish are you on?"

"The last one," Autar answered, and refused to take a set himself.

"What?" Madison utters the sound so quick I almost don't even register the word. "Did you wish to give up wishes after the gold thing?"

"The gold thing," Autar repeated with a sigh, "was the third and final wish. We actually wished he'd stop drinking."

"Oh." He said nothing more as Henri is still studying the gold wine glass. "Wait, no. What is this *final* business?"

If he makes me explain all three wishes, I'm going to die of embarrassment. Only to likely be brought back and want to die all over again. "The rule of three states that's how much power a jinn has."

"Like magical edging?" Madison asked as his head tilts. "Not to shame how you play, but the lamp had nine masters, making you the 10th. They'd be too much… time full of nothing if that was true. Connections between people break if not ever invoked."

Thankfully, Henri changed the topic as Autar looks too embarrassed to speak. "Where did you hear that you could only get three wishes?"

"I…" *Where did we hear that?* It was just something everyone heard as a kid. Three is a magic number. Just like the sky is blue.

"I really don't mean to push, the mmm…," Madison said, struggling with the thought. His hand tapped Henri's knee as he found the phrasing. "Relationship between you two. But magic grows stronger with repeated usage.

Between a master and jinn, a better bond makes wishes stronger. Your first wish was easy to break, because it inherently keep you apart."

Henri looked to each of us. "How is that pushing a relationship?"

"They aren't together, love."

"Ah." His expression grew sympathetic even as he fights back a laugh and rubbed his eyes. They clearly know what's going on so much better than us and that still made me slightly furious.

"What was the second wish?" Henri followed up, innocently enough, and I absolutely was not going to answer. Or allow Autar to answer if he even could stop being tinted with a blush.

"Doesn't matter," I said. "Just this gold thing is lasting. Unlike the other wishes we made. An endless supply of gold could ruin economies with a sudden influx of wealth."

Madison snickered. Henri glanced over to him before taking a deep breath and seemed far more willing to talk geopolitics with me. "Easy solution for you," he said. "Stop trying to drink."

"As we were telling you," Autar said, as he crossed his arms. "Our actual problem is–"

"All those people," Madison interrupted, with more giggling. "Hoarding gold and thinking they are wealthy only to have you accidentally ruin it all."

"Mads, love," Henri said softly.

"Hmm?"

"Please go distract yourself, you're putting them off."

Madison lifted a couple fingers to the brim of his hat, as if to signal a goodbye, then headed down the hall to their bedroom.

"See? I'm a magical oddity," I started off, but something thumped against my boot. A glance down to my foot reveals another wine bottle had been rolled my way. Autar's breath hitched, not expecting the shiver of magic. The worst thing is I don't even want to drink right now, and the uncorked bottle still glittered into gold. "This is exactly what I mean! What if we are found and made to do this under a worse context?"

My least favorite person was sitting on the floor at the end of the hallway. Hat sitting next to him, with his tongue out as if carefully trying to aim each bottle of their wine collection at me. I knew I wasn't allowed to harm him, but I could try to show how ridiculous the prince's husband had been.

Autar leaned forward so he could see what was going on. "Oddly fun, right?" he said, and the Hatter nodded back.

"Please help me," I begged, and realized it hadn't been for the first time.

"I'm not enabling your alcoholism," Henri said sternly. "Learn magic, and it will probably happen more situationally."

This tactic would never work. I had to ask for help in a way that would actually result in getting it. Just like how this home had been given to them 'situationally'. I cleared my throat then asked, "Which one of you faked your death this time to end up here?" There had to be some honor between magical outlaws. If not, maybe blackmail would work.

"Neither of us," Henri said, only sitting back in his seat over the shift in my tone. "Shortly after you were exiled, we decided to leave. The ruling didn't sit right with us, neither did the war. So, we reminded the powers that be that I am already legally dead, and that Madison can body swap on his own command."

"A veteran's debt to the kingdom is considered paid," Autar said, shifting back to a neutral gray. "Upon the death of their spouse. You married before you fought with us."

Those two mages were dangerously clever. I had been right about them being tricksters, just wrong about their motives. They just wanted to be together and free. No fault in that dream.

Autar mumbled something under his breath. I couldn't even hear it but the sound alone made me grimace. If we had stayed together, gotten married, we too could have had a peacefully calm life in this little retiree community.

But no. Of course not. We hadn't shared the same dreams and understanding. Even the rule of three was bullshit that we self-imposed on ourselves.

"Hey!" Madison yelled from down the hall. When I glanced over, I couldn't see him anymore, yet I still got the feeling that he was trying to help out somehow. "Why is my watch all melty?"

Autar grimaced. "About that…"

"Come here, please," he first said in singsong. "Hadi doesn't like me."

Autar glanced at me, then laughed before heading into the bedroom.

I wanted to deny it. Especially since my gut feeling was jealousy. As if it was even reasonable to be worried about Madison touching Autar. Wait… *could they?* The watch didn't look damaged to me anymore, and Autar hadn't mentioned it being off still.

"Starting to see why you were drinking," Henri commented from the couch.

"Thank you," I said, feeling vindicated.

The feeling of kinship quickly evaporated as he shook

his head. "You are wound up and have no outlet. Often why I used to drink."

"And now?"

"I like liquor and my husband."

Why did the Hatter leave Autar that pocket watch? Had he always expected him to return? Had they been waiting? *Oh, fuck this.* I got up and decided to see what they were doing back there.

"Face your fears," Henri added, as I stood and pretended I didn't hear him.

The two of them sat on the edge of the bed, shoulder to shoulder. Autar looked like this had been his only spot, and Madison was the one to move closer, still just slightly further back.

Their hands were empty, but I couldn't bring myself to look where the watch was because they *were* touching. It wasn't obscene, but still oddly intimate as Madison's hand was on Autar's wrist.

"What's—" I managed to mumble before my throat tightened and cut off the question.

"I wasn't talking to you," Madison said, eyes flicking up to me. I had been so focused on hating him outright, I hadn't even stopped to realize what he could do to me if he disliked me back. "I'm in the middle of an apology here."

I wanted to figure out what in the world he was sorry about but had to first convince my body that I could still breath through my nose. In the absence of my words I could hear his softly spoken ones.

"Sorry, I didn't realize you thought the wishes were limited. Figured by time you found the watch, found me, you'd be so used to holding magic that it wouldn't have done that to you."

Autar nodded slightly as he stared at the ground. There was no way he didn't know I was here and even tightly closed his eyes as if better able to avoid me. If I lost Autar, I'd deserve it. A brief stint of trying to put him first and sobriety didn't repair everything.

"Must have been scary," Madison continued softly. "To be free of a body that's been holding you back, and then feel like even that's poisoned and not know why."

Autar glanced up to the roof, eyes glossy and trying to hold it back.

"I'm sorry," Madison said again, giving Autar's wrist another little squeeze. How was someone as powerful as him so capable of admitting his wrongs? "I've been trying to do better with my blessings. Not leave people high and dry, give them a way to get help if they need."

Madison's sharp eyes caught me again and I tried swallowing but the lump in my throat only piled up. I should have stayed back with Henri. "Do you want to be free of him? Does he help?"

"Yeah." Autar's eyes fell to mine, and I've never been more afraid of anything in my life. "He helps."

"I'm glad," Madison said, and the tightness in my throat eased. I could probably speak again if I could think of anything worthy enough to say. "Do you want me to mess with his head some more? Might be able to make him more talkative."

Autar smiled. "No, thank you. He's pretty alright how he is."

Chapter Seventeen

Something inside me broke when he said those words. "I can be better. I'll do better. For you." Once I had the words, I was worried about losing them, and they flowed out in a ramble. "You're my best friend. Anything you need."

Autar's surprised expression shifted quickly towards annoyance somewhere along the way. He stood up, as I willed myself perfectly still. "Learn to take care of yourself."

He pushed past, shoulder checking me on his way out. It was such a common way to start a fight that we never actually had. But this time, instead of angry I was stunned. We could touch again?

Autar realized this afterward as well, movement stalling out for a moment before he continued out into the hallway.

"What did you do to him?" I growled.

"You need to learn to when to stay back." Madison rose up to his knees on the bed, it was an odd pose for such a serious statement. "And when to chase after someone."

"What did you do to him?" I repeated the demand.

"What did *you* do to him?" he countered. "Get out."

In a huff, I turned and headed for the front door. "Come on Autar, we are leaving."

"Why?"

I was so annoyed I couldn't even pick out if that was Henri's or Autar's voice. When I looked back, Henri was the one standing, holding his hand out low as if asking Autar to stay.

"We were asked to leave."

"No, you weren't," Henri said, and I don't think he had overheard anything. "And if you were, I'm telling you to stay. You can't just run away from a murder scene, hide here, then flee nowhere."

Autar and Henri must have talked further themselves since he knew about the people after us.

"Your husband says otherwise." I crossed my arms over my chest. Why was this even being debated? "Let's go."

"I'll talk to him," Henri said, holding my glare until I relented and sat down. "You two talk as well." This time he didn't wait until I complied before leaving.

"I want to stay," Autar said, even if his voice didn't seem strong right now. "At least for tonight. I'm tired of trying to go this alone. Feeling as if we are on the run, like I'm your dirty little secret."

"You're not–" I started to say, but caught myself this time. I had been making things about myself when I shouldn't, and *not* making them about myself when I should.

I never considered what it might mean for Autar to be touched again. By anyone. Just assumed it still mattered less to him than to me. So it mustn't be that important if I could go without it.

"You want me sober for me," I said, feeling stupid, but pushing on anyway. "To be better, for me."

Autar nodded. Not saying anything for a long moment. And I was glad he didn't want me to be more talkative because I'm happy he was often quiet too. It's what made me feel at peace and comfortable together.

"If there had been only three wishes, if my lamp gets taken, or we got separated somehow. There'd be solace in knowing you'd be okay. I know we are friends, Hadi. I know, but I really care about you."

I wasn't cursed, I was blessed. Deeply so. "I'll learn to care about me too."

Henri stepped back in. "He meant get out of our bedroom. You were crowding him."

"How was I meant to know that?"

"You ask," Henri said, and I felt incredibly daft there was such a simple answer. Henri grabbed some cups and placed them on the table. "Would you like some tea?"

"I can't," Autar said, frowning.

"Why not? Surely you still don't have food problems as a jinn?" Henri asked as he started preparing tea. "I don't have to be able to touch you for you to pick it up."

His gaze lowered. "My hand phases through most things."

"Even during golden hour?"

"During what?" I felt suddenly warm all over. Was time tied to the wish? Could there be more moments than just magic calling to magic?

"Golden hour?" Henri checked. "It's the first hour after sunrise and the last hour of light before sunset. Mads mentioned you touched. You should probably ask him to explain things more thoroughly next time."

What did you do to him?' Our wish. It had lucky timing.

And magical wordplay gave us everything we wanted.

"What type of tea is it?" Autar asked with a hopeful smile. His fingers slowly reached out to the warm teacup. Flinching back for a moment as his skin registered the heat.

"It's a miracle," I mumbled and reached my hand over to touch Autar's arm. "Your wishes are miracles."

"It's a limited one," Autar laughed, his hand pausing on mine and gently lifting my hand off with a slight squeeze. "I'd like to try whatever tea this is."

"Right." I took my own tea as it brewed so my hands would have something to hold on to.

"Afraid I don't know what's inside this brew," Henri answered, and the cup held it under his nose to tell by smell. "It's part of the rations we are given."

"It's sage," Autar answered, as the cup lowered from his lips.

"Are you hungry?" Henri asked, glancing at both of us. "If you have a longing for anything we don't have, I can probably fish it from Mads' hat."

"Baskot wa-raha, actually," Autar said, and Henri continued to listen not recognizing that name. "It's two cookies between a powered confection. Not even that good, really. Just feeling nostalgic. Oh, but please don't trouble yourself. I don't want to have to choose between them and my drink."

Henri grinned, probably finding him as cute as I did. I think Autar just enjoyed being asked. "I'll find some later," I said, and he shot me a funny look. "What? I like them too. A man needs to eat."

"I'll have to try them sometime," Henri said. "Since they are such a group favorite."

Autar smiled. Wider than I'd seen in a long time. Jinn, or

not. And the trio of us fell into a comfortable conversation as we went on past the golden hour and into the night.

Someone's gasp woke me up in the morning. My eyes struggled to adjust to the low light enough to see smoke spilling out of the bottle as if throwing him up.

Autar righted himself enough to stand, eyes wide as they search the room for danger before his gaze falls to his wrists. He rubbed over the area with one hand, then the other.

"What's the matter?" I asked from the couch. It's still before sunrise, I can tell by how little light is peaking through the curtains.

"I—" His chest is letting out uneven breaths until he takes a moment to calm himself. "I thought my hands were shackled."

"Bad dream?"

"No. I mean… I don't know. It felt so real. I think trouble is coming."

I frowned, not because I don't believe him, but because I don't know what to do about it. If we were part of the guard, we'd have plans ready. He's never woken up randomly from a nightmare before so I'm not sure what he might need even if it's a false alarm.

Madison quickly walked out of his room as if on a mission. He turned to Autar as if surprised we were still here. "Did you feel it too?"

Autar just nodded, and the combination makes me sure something is wrong with the world.

"I need to wake Henri," Madison mumbled and is headed back.

"Wait! What should we do?"

Without even looking back he yelled, "Listen to your jinn!"

I glance over to Autar with a strained smile.

He shrugged. "I'll check around for any booze?"

"You don't have to do that. I'm good. Really." I definitely don't need to be taken care of, especially in this second.

"Look, just because you can't physically drink anymore, I don't want you to suffer the pain of reaching for it knowing you might've caved in if you could have. That's not good for you either." Despite his seriousness, I'm smiling softly. "Also, he said listen to me. Maybe someone's coming for more gold."

Honestly hadn't thought of that. "You're so smart, my memory is goldfish level."

Autar sways, giving me a careful look before checking the area for alcohol and then hiding the bottles he finds between sheets in a linen closet. He's able to move them, so it must be what is needed at the moment. I hope next time he gets a laugh out of someone drinking I'm in on the joke.

Henri came out of his room, and instead of positioning himself behind us for protection, paced across the front windows. Once invisible glyphs shined with bright wards as he lent his magic to charge them. When he turns back towards the door, a hand swiped away and only that symbol faded away. "Apologies for not guaranteeing your safety within our home. But we don't know who or what is coming and need the answer to both questions."

Madison's eyes are closed, leaning against the hallway

wall. Back turned to whatever is coming. "Untuned mage, funneling towards the door. Just the one. Carrying, or wearing, silver."

I grabbed my bag from the floor where I'd been sleeping and held the bundled-up lamp out to Henri. "Can you protect this? We trust you."

Henri glanced over to Autar as if to check if he agreed and was given a certain nod. "Of course. With everything I have."

The former prince stepped back, and I take up the space, positioned in front. Madison hasn't moved an inch but smiles approvingly when I make eye contact. There's not much room, even for my short blade if I still had it, but I'm still determined to do my part. A fighter still, through and through.

The door's lock is slowly picked, normally I wouldn't have even realized such a thing made a sound. Expecting us all asleep, a man crept in. Quickly rising to his whole height when he sees all of us standing in wait.

Autar's guess was right. The previously unknown danger *was* targeting me because, after quick look over us all, he lashed out at me. Not attempting any sidestep towards jinn, lamp, or closest mage.

I caught the wrist of his weaponed hand, using my added weight to throw him down on the ground. As I kick the silver knife away, the assassin bites down on something between his teeth.

Spit bubbled out of his mouth, and Madison's hand darted over. The stranger's seizing stopped as if time was held frozen. The only movement is that of bubbles receding. I lose what's happening as the necromancer sticks his fingers in the man's mouth, then pulls out a small intact pill. "Not so quick with your death there," Madison cooed.

Just when I think things can go back to the realm of normal, the pill is placed between his front teeth. Madison bit down, then spit onto the floor. Thankfully, I'm not the only one mortified by him. Autar is wide-eyed, and Henri is standing there with a hand on his chest.

"What?" Madison asked, as if not understanding what he just did. "It was the pill's time, not his."

"God, you're terrifying," I confessed.

Henri tiredly sighed, but his husband beamed over my words. "That's so kind, thank you."

I think we might be friends now. Guess I could be an adult about that fact too. "Now what do we do?"

If I'm freaked out by the assassin that had been sent, he is absolutely the one most in shock. The one and only escape he had if captured ruined and cornered by a trio of wildly powerful casters. And me, someone who would absolutely bleed before letting anything happen to any of them.

"The lawful thing would be to turn him in. Have the local authorities deal with him," Madison explained. The man under his hold tried to jerk free but gained nothing but a firmer grip for the effort. "But the former guard captain is my houseguest, so I'm asking for permission to use the faster method."

"Sure?" I wanted Autar to keep his freedom, for their home to stay safe for them. Hell, I don't want to be die by some stranger's authority either.

Without a word, the assassin convulses for a moment as his eyes roll up on his head. Madison's eyes also closed and I'm not quite sure what I just allowed.

"Who was he after?" Henri asked and laced his fingers with Madison's free hand, who was slow to hold it back.

"There's such a story here. I'm not sure where to start," Madison explained, eyelids moving as if dreaming.

"You're anchored to me, I got you," Henri added, voice not betraying how nervous he actually looked. "Start a week ago. What do you see?"

"The Beast. He's grown angry, impatient, wants…." Madison cocked his head as he loses the thought. "Wants what?"

The assassin let out a low groan, whatever magic is going on, it's not comfortable for either of them.

"Love," Madison answered finally. For a moment, I think he's talking to Henri. "The Wolf King. Death. Mastery of jinn."

He opened his eyes calmly, a stark comparison to the assassin who fell forward panting. He's free, almost ignored for the time being, but looked in no shape to flee now. "Bernard here was sent by Prince Adam to kill Hadi for the lamp."

Madison hits Bernard upside the head. "Why'd you hold someone else's secrets so tightly? Made it hurt for the both of us! You were an open book in comparison. Just pushing thoughts forward to try to throw me off. Thinking you're so weird having a rape kink. Grow the fuck up, get a safe word. All that personal information that I did not ask for."

I hated that if our situations had been reversed, if Jasmine sent me on a mission where my memories were picked apart for information about her? I also would have held onto her secrets, her everything before my own anything. And the longer I protected someone else over myself, the more it would have hurt.

"You okay?" Autar asked me. Despite looking upset himself that people have at least suggested taking the lamp twice in as many days.

"Besides learning that a Prince of Heart I never met wants me dead? Yeah, I'm great." The strangest thing about this whole day was that I weirdly meant it. We were okay. We were all together. "How did someone so far away even hear I have it?"

"Because Prince Sorry-Can't-Go-My-Town-Needs-Me is on the move. That's also why this was a kill-or-be-killed type mission. The Beast doesn't want anyone to know they were already in town when they heard about jinn magic. He was originally looking for the Wolf King before he got greedy."

Autar backed up out of the circle we were standing in. Suddenly looked like he didn't want to be a part of this conversation and all of its talk of murder, magic, and kink. I think he might have had a panic attack if he had actual lungs.

Then the sun rose, and his breathing wavered and either way Autar was going to have one.

"I got this," Henri said and picked the Bernard up by the arm. He wasn't as strong as Madison, but the man yelped and quickly stopped fighting as they pulled him outside to avoid more pain. Figuring they could handle it, I turned to focus on Autar.

"Hey, you're safe," I whispered. "Probably safer than ever actually."

He laughed nervously, knowing it was a joke in a way and truth in others. But it didn't seem to help.

My hand lifted, wondering if he would rather be touched. *I* wanted to touch him, hold him, pull him close, and not let him go for anything.

"Oh please, don't touch me right now," Autar whined.

My hand dropped in an instant. Able to touch or not. Didn't matter. I listened and did not take the moment personally. "You got it."

"I'm not used to being the one someone wants," he confessed. I wish could empathize with what that felt like, but I only knew what being someone's shield felt like. We both only had until now.

"Sounds scary."

"Yeah…"

"I'm here. And for, however long it's my choice, I'll never go anywhere."

"Yeah?"

I nodded. "Wouldn't want to be anywhere else, no matter what."

Some time passed in silence as Autar stayed inside, still quietly panicking, and I started to wonder what the mages were doing. But do nothing besides crane my neck to glance out the crack in the blinds.

"Hadi?"

I turned my full attention back to him. "What is it, habib?"

He seemed stunned once again. I think calling him beloved threw him off further. Can't remember the last time I've done it, even though he let it slip several times casually since we broke up. Even in the guard. It's not an overtly romantic term to begin with. I fear I've hurt him further before he crashes into me with his arms thrown over my shoulders.

"I just really needed that hug now," he mumbled into my shoulder. *Oh my god,* it might be the best hug I've ever had. My arms wrapped around him; all I know is that I'm not going to be the one who pulls away first this time.

Chapter Eighteen

"Do you have any change?" Madison asked as he's tossing cushions and checking under furniture. If he keeps going, he's going to find the wine soon.

What I wanted to say is, 'yes, everything's changed in my life.' But I'm sure he literally means coins right now. And I did not have any. "No, why?"

"Damn it," Madison grumbled, and walked into his bedroom. Maybe to look under the mattress or something.

"Mads, love?" Henri called from the hallway. "Were you hiding wine from me?"

"Course not. Hadi's the alcoholic, remember?" he yelled back.

Autar shook his head. "Why don't you give Hadi the wine? I will turn it into gold, then Henri can melt it down and you can turn the metal into gold coins."

"That's—" I'm pretty sure he's about to call Autar brilliant but stopped short to think it through. "No, that won't work. I need the essence of monetary sovereignty."

I don't have that either, so I look down at the tied and

gagged would-be assassin on the floor in front of me. His eyes are wide and pleading for me to be the reasonable one. This is definitely not how he expected his afternoon to go. Doesn't even get the sexy version of this going super weird either. "They are a bit much, right?"

He nodded eagerly back. Mumbling something as the scarf in his mouth is murdering the words too much.

"Tell me about it," I replied all the same. "Honestly? The weirdly wondrous magic grows on you. It's more about the people you are with anyway, you know?"

He sighed heavily, likely realizing his target was not here to help him. After a glance towards Autar, who has been glaring daggers at him, his shoulders deflate even further.

"Okay, look," Madison said, coming to a stop in front of me. "You don't have to go home, but you can't stay here. I need a favor."

Henri walked over too, taking a seat next to Autar. They can't touch since the sun is too high in the sky. But the mage can still see him, so Henri nods an acknowledgment and Autar doesn't need to move from his spot. It's enough to be seen.

Madison snapped his fingers in front of my face. "Focus, please."

"Good grief," I mumbled, being nearly forced to take a step back with his closeness. "What's the favor?"

"You need to get out of town. I want to warn the Wolf King. Two birds, one stone." Madison glanced to the side, maybe wondering if a stone would work before he is shaking his head. "The problem is I don't know how to find him."

Autar had mentioned leaving town before this and can't say there's anything here for me. "Sure." I nod over at our prisoner. "What about him?"

"Henri can offer him to Princess Jasmine. I'm sure she won't like Prince Adam trying to kill even an outlaw on her land."

"No, she won't," Henri agreed as if we didn't know that even more than them. "Prince Adam's bark is usually worse than his bite." That I didn't know and hope for our sake it's still true.

"If we need you again, how do we find you?" Autar asked. If he could have, I think he might have also hugged them both.

"You won't," Madison answered.

It takes Henri's hand on Madison's arm for me to realize he'd been trying to be reassuring. "But we aren't going anywhere," Henri added.

We first go to collect our stuff at the abandoned guard tower. Wind slipped through the broken wall, pulling the torn curtains out like a flag. The castle itself still sits there, as regal and pristine as ever.

"Worried about the war?" Autar asked.

I shook my head. "The guard is full of good people. We trained them the best we could. They'll handle it, and hopefully, it won't go on much longer."

"Do you still miss it?"

I took a moment. Certain he meant not only leading the guard but the castle itself and all of its comforts. In some ways, it would always be home. "Less than before." This seemed to please him as he smiled a little, which makes me smile back.

The most important things were in my bag already. But we couldn't forget Autar's few things and any food I had left before we headed out. It didn't feel like enough to make it far, but anything more and we risked the bag spilling.

Outsiders complained about our deserts, but I've always preferred it compared to the forests that line the rest of Wonderland. When a landscape is flat, one can see where they are going. Know that they are making progress. See what lies ahead.

A forest? With flaking bark, falling leaves, and branches snapping underfoot. Who knew what you'd find, or what would find you.

I dropped my bag and almost collapsed in the first grassy clearing big enough to set up camp. The soil was spongy with moss underneath me. Here was good enough for today.

Autar's neck craned up, looking at the canopy above us. "I don't think I've ever seen trees this tall before."

They weren't dreadfully different from the type back home, but the cooler weather brought out changes that made everything far more yellow. "I bet the view from above is even more remarkable. You could probably float your way up there."

"Do you mind?"

I shook my head and watched with a small smile as his magical smoke rode upwards within the breeze.

Chapter Nineteen

"Why do you keep doing that?"

"Doing what?" I haven't the faintest clue what he is talking about. I've been nothing but a diligent aid as we packed up camp, hiked, then set up again for the night. Alright, maybe I *did* know what I was doing.

"Being… obedient," he said. "I'm used to you being a leader."

My tongue darted over my bottom lip, barely able to hold back the question, *'but do you like it?'* If we could only touch twice a day, I'd be more than happy to work for it. Instead, I focus on why he asked in the first place. "Just realized you could now kick my ass if you wanted. Need to show you the amount of respect that deserves, so you don't."

He grinned. "You're so full of it."

"Full of what?"

"I don't know," he said, distracted with setting up. There are specific things he can still do, and others that I can do far easier. In a lot of ways, it reminded me of how we coped with his disabilities before.

"But whatever it is," Autar continued, "You're full up."

I laughed, the feeling a pleased earthquake in my chest. Didn't realize not drinking could feel this nice. "I don't think that makes sense."

"You don't make sense," Autar mumbled, hanging a canvas cloth over a tree branch the bed roll will rest under.

I end up doing more than my share and end up kicking things in the right direction to save time. There's something not being said, and I can feel it hanging in the air.

"You are always so preoccupied with things I couldn't do, or things I didn't want to do as much as you. That you neglected to ask what I wanted. Which is to help you, to be at your side. The lamp changed a lot, but not that."

"Should we really be having this conversation now?"

"If we are tied together, maybe until death do us part, I want to talk about this."

The words felt stuck in my throat. With a grunt, I spit the thought out. "You're right. I wanted to protect you, and each time that didn't happen, I blamed myself. So, I pushed you away. Then you were turned into a jinn and I could have truly lost you." I wanted to grab his face up in my hands but knew I'd find it still wispy under my fingers. "But you're still here," I said. The fact that this is even possible is beautiful. "So, who cares if there's an afterlife? Because you're here now."

Autar's eyes widened like he couldn't believe what he heard, then his expression broke into a light laugh. "I forgot how sweet you are sober. Hope I get to put up with it for a long time."

We lived off the land. Chopping wood and otherwise acting like the bears we always were at heart. Time was a funny thing to the Hatter so we didn't push to get anywhere specific fast. We had no location, so taking our time was less of a detour than it was enjoying the journey.

"I wish I could cook for you." My voice softly carried over the fire long after the sun has set. "Make sure you got everything you needed without you even having to think about it. But I'd probably get distracted by you, and let things burn."

Autar's smiling at outlandish, domestic as all get out, ideal that we will never have. "And then what?"

"You'd discipline me for the mess I made."

A corner of his mouth quirked up. "You'd love every minute of that."

I nodded, lips parting to form a smile I can't seem to keep off my face.

"Can't stand this," Autar complained but doesn't seem bothered until he sighed roughly before speaking again. "I'm afraid to even say what I wish. That we'll cause even more magical fuckery in this world."

"It's just you and me right now. I'll wait all night if you'd be more comfortable. Nothing matters more to me."

"When the light breaks in the morning," Autar said, glancing towards the horizon as if to watch for the sun before his keen eyes find mine again. "I will have you."

If I could bottle the intensity in his eyes, we'd be able to rule all the lands. But that would mean I'd have to share even more of our precious second chance together. "I'm yours," I said, voice a whisper in the night. "For as long as you want."

"Until dawn, beg."

My eyes widen in alarm, wanting to cave sooner but I'm happy to hold firm. I swallowed roughly. This is such a good look on him. Like he knows he's the most powerful being around.

"That's not a wish," Autar added. "It's a guarantee of what's going to happen. Let me hear your every desire."

I watched closely as he inhales, but no magic compelled him further. "Yes, Master."

We couldn't fully resist each other until morning. And ended up working on inventive ways to skirt the rules on the whole only one hour twice a day aspect. It quickly stopped being anything like our drunken quick fixes. More so, a night full of intermixed bursts of excitement when we figured something new out.

Autar shivered as I stepped back, the new distance seemingly important to him as my anxiety only grew. "You've never reacted to my touch like that before," I said, realizing the flaw. "Or rather, lack of touch."

There was still time left before we could directly touch, but if careful enough, we could tug on the other's clothes. Anything that could be removed didn't seem to count as the other, so long as we avoided direct pressure. It made the lightest sensations maddeningly heightened.

"Everything feels…" Autar started but ended up shaking his head a little. "You wouldn't understand."

"No." The sound was without thought as his frown made the rest of my words stumble out. "But I want to. Please, go on."

"It's all so magical. You'd think I'd feel it less between

golden hours." Autar looked down at his hands, solid, whole, strong. "But I feel it even more. As if magic is made in moments like this."

"What?" I snorted. "Foreplay?"

"No, or rather, not exclusively." Autar frowned more as he spoke. "More so when I feel close to you. When there's trust between us."

"There's always trust between us."

"Not like this," he breathed.

I watched the sunrise in the reflection of his eyes. Autar must have been watching the horizon too because my heart skipped when he finally caught my gaze.

It's as if the world doesn't exist outside our bodies. *Well, my body seeing as...*

"Hadi." There's humor in his light scolding. "Stop thinking."

"Why does it seem like you can read my mind now?"

"It's nothing magical. You tense up, it's noticeable in someone your size. Especially since I also know how relaxed you occasionally can allow yourself."

"I'll be better at that."

"Good," Autar roughly said. "You'll have time later to prove it to me this evening."

I grumbled to myself over the fact that I had the best night of my life, without finishing once and didn't want to stop now. Seemed unfair on the surface, but I'd absolutely do it again. In a heartbeat. Even if it ended exactly the same. I'm not exactly sure what time it is, but I'm also tired and hungry so I first make myself breakfast.

Sometime in the evening, we lost our sexy domestic play banter, and started to talk about more serious things. Not working all day, eating three meals, and the lack of drinking kept causing replies to pop into my head. Making me equally to blame for keeping the conversation going. Maybe this topic was just overdue, and we had the time now.

"Don't you think I saw, Hadi? Witnessed every time you fell apart, got lost in your own head. Able to do nothing but try to cover for you. Sometimes pretend that even I didn't know what a mess you were, just so you'd have something to hold on to. Even if that something was just a sense of vain pride?"

"I'm sorry."

"We know each other. That's why we are still here," Autar said, moving throughout the camp, the gravelly patch of ground under him turning no stones over with his lack of actual footfall. "I'm here because I want to be."

"I'm sorry," I found myself repeating.

"No, I'm not accepting that answer. Dig deeper."

"What?"

"Tell me what you are actually feeling, under the pain."

"I…" Even with a glance around the campsite, all I can really focus on is that I've led armies, helped plan cities, and yet *this* is the hardest undertaking ever asked. "I'm grateful," the word comes out as a sob. "And just so blessed you are still here."

"The only reason I want this is because it's you."

I froze. Autar had said those words to me before and I felt just as panicked as I did then. "Because of the magical bond? I don't—"

"*I do.*" He placed a hand under my chin and lifts it. "Can't you trust me to do what I please?"

His touch is so normal, and absolutely the best thing in

the world right now. His hand isn't soft, it is still calloused. Good thing my heart isn't counting the seconds because it would beat too fast and lose several. "It's an hour until sunset."

Autar grinned. "It is."

"I'm excited you're into this."

He pulled his hand back but didn't step away. "I've always been into anything you suggest. You're the one that's always held back."

"No way, come on." Now that my mind is clear, I realize how right he is. I am the one who thought I'd break him, feared I was taking advantage. Sometimes even that he was the one not giving me something when he always offered everything I ever asked of him.

Our relationship failed, not because he lacked *anything*, but because I had always been incapable of asking for what I wanted. I scooped Autar's face into my hands, kissing him tenderly, leaving him confused by the softness of it. Shoulders tensing as if to balance us out.

A breath later, he asked, "What was that for?"

I laughed, and at this moment I understood how love can make us all mad. "Just realized how right you've always been. I can't imagine what I'd be without you."

"Then don't."

My stomach fluttered. I don't think it's anything I've eaten. And the first thought I have to avoid the feeling from consuming me whole is the safe word we had almost jokingly started off with making. "Cranberries."

"What?"

"It's my safe word, remember?" *Stars, I'm still fucking nervous.* Maybe I used it wrong somehow. "I said it was fitting because they aren't native here, so it's not like I'd randomly see one."

"Babe," he said patiently and clearly not trying to laugh as he bit his tongue, making himself pause. "I'm not touching you."

"Right." We'd just been standing there. Even after *I* let go of his face, we weren't extremely close. "Sorry."

"It's okay," he said softly, and I believed him. The sun is still setting, and it doesn't matter because there are going to be other days. "Are you feeling any better?"

"Yes, thank you."

Autar nodded as he tended to the fire. Wood had proved odd when it's not a golden hour, he can only seem to pick it up when the fire is growing low. Rope, however, seemed workable anytime. It's very strange to me and I wonder if we'll ever figure each other fully out. "Autar?" I called over.

"Huh?" He glanced up, clearly expecting me to give an order. That's the rule. I give the orders when we aren't fooling around.

But it's technically still golden hour, and I really want to touch him. I groaned, knowing I'm the one who still needs to grow up and admit my most embarrassing desires. "Can we... cuddle?"

"Oh stars, you scared me," he said, exhaling all at once. "It's been... the longest day. I'd like really that."

We spend the remaining light in each other's arms, and fall asleep, only to wake up, curled up in each other's warmth as the sun rose again.

There's no schedule so we make no push to get today started. I sit up, grinning to myself as I run my finger up Autar's happy trial. The hairs bending to follow before his shirt ends my path.

"What are you smirking about?" he asked lazily.

"Just failed to appreciate every part of you before."

"Let's not make the same mistakes again." It's a more serious tone than before, but I deserve it.

"I won't."

He turned over, more on his back, to look up at me. "I won't either."

What error did he ever make? "You being sick or anything else was never your fault."

Autar shook his head. "No, but I let you always command. Always be the leader. I let go of us, as if it was an order you gave."

I pulled him close, nuzzling my head into the crook of his neck. "How much time this morning?"

"Not long."

"That's okay."

We travel through the forests during the day, stopping with enough daylight left to set up camp. Fire is the trickiest for us. I brought no proper tools, and Autar's magic can't seem to spark a smoking ember. I task myself with sticks and friction knowing with patience it's possible to start a fire.

"Oh the situations, rope has gotten us into," Autar mused, as he looped it several times around a tree to serve as an anchor. If I let him continue, the other end will be thrown over another tree up at an angle and tied to our food cache, so wild animals are kept away at the night.

I wondered if he was thinking about when we climbed

down into that cave. Would be the most fitting, innocent thought. But can't claim that's where my mind is as I watch him pull the length of rope between his hands. "I was kind of hungry for something else."

By this point, one end is already secured, and he glanced down to the other, searching for my meaning. "Think you're brave enough?"

"You know I'm brave enough for anything."

Autar lifted a brow. "Then ask."

His words held back, tantalizing me with the unsaid prompt. Forcing me to be the one to cave first. "Rather have you show me."

He took a few steps toward me, slow and almost predatory. "Be careful what you wish for."

Have I ever? "You probably could tie me up if you were careful. We wouldn't even have to touch."

"We should test this," Autar said, gaze holding mine. "For research."

"Yes." I swallowed, excitement already building. "How else will we know?"

The combination of gravity and distance become my new best friends. The combination of their aid is what allows Autar to drop the rope around then step back to have it tighten.

I can't feel his hands on me, but instead the vibration through the rope as his hands run over it. I tug a bit at the binds at my back. There's limited slack giving me some mobility if I wanted to drop on my knees, or even take a step to either side.

"What are you feeling right now?" Autar asked.

"What do you mean?" *How do I answer that besides the*

obvious?

His hands lifted away but didn't go far as they hovered under my bound wrists. It's such a soft ritualistic gesture beneath the tight intricate ties that allowed us to avoid skin contact. "The threads between us aren't gold right now. They are red. Thought maybe it shifted with your feelings."

"You're here too," I answered, and what a lovely answer it was. "What are you feeling right now?"

When he made eye contact, I expect to be scolded for avoiding the question. But he's still smiling. "I feel happy."

"Gold's a soft metal," I playfully reminded as he had before. "Maybe we wore through to something stronger underneath."

"Don't forget this one key thing," he said, "The sun doesn't decide when we are through: *We do.*"

I nodded; eyes full of stars, even though it was just him filling my vision. "I love you," I confessed because it always sounds like one to me. Not a mere fact, not a hope, nor even an old promise. But a feeling locked deep inside that I'll never be free from. And I'm not afraid of that acknowledgment anymore.

He stepped around towards the stack behind me, hand running along the rope the whole way. "I never stopped." After his own confession, he yanked at the rope, and I stumbled back towards the tree.

"Do you know why I'm punishing you right now?" Autar asked, stepping maddeningly just out of my peripheral vision.

I haven't even caught my breath after being thrown off. "Because I'm a fuckup who ruins everything?"

He stepped into view, lips pursed together, trying not to smile. "No, try again."

I swallowed roughly, wishing he'd just hurt me instead. Pain was a familiar feeling, vulnerability was not. "Because I still think it's deserved," I answered, gritting my teeth, words slowly released after being buried for years. "And I only want to find justice by your hands."

He took a step, possibly to control the rope, but I didn't want him out of my sight again. My chest finally felt lighter, and I didn't want to stop. "I don't care about some royal's stupid war when we have each other."

"You've been so good tonight," Autar rewarded. His hand ran through my hair, gripping hard at its length. Yet only relief floods my senses. The fact that I could feel pain at all from him pulling my hair is a wonder. "What else is the war?"

"Oh so, petty."

Autar grabbed my jaw, pulling my mouth to his mouth. The kiss is brushing, and I can't get enough of it. If I had my way, my lips wouldn't leave his salty skin for the entire hour.

Our travels follow a comfortable pattern that might not last beyond the forest's edges, but actively enjoyable for the time being. Sleep, travel, play.

I strained against the restraints, with only one want left, one specific question filling my mind. "What are you waiting for now?"

Autar smirked as he looked over at me, exceedingly proud of his handy work looped intricately around me. "You know exactly what I'm waiting for."

My eyes dart to the horizon, the sun is still in the sky refusing even think of setting yet. I test the restraints hold until it bites back.

"Absolutely no way you're getting out of that," Autar purred, utterly enjoying himself already. "You're going to have to wait for it."

"Couldn't you maybe use some magic? Speed up the time." I'm absolutely not above begging if it's what it takes.

"Keep talking that way, and I'm going to cut your time," he warned.

"Forgive me. Punish me, whatever you want, but anything but *that.*"

The pleading earned a smirk, and I now valued open communication above all else. Autar must be able to feel the shift within him because, unlike me, he doesn't need to watch the sun to know when golden hour starts. His hand grazed against my beard like the beginning of a dream. "We have an hour," he said like a prayer. "You ready?"

Nodded, so eager that I will my mouth shut in case I say something to ruin this moment. My newfound love of words is not needed at this exact second.

His hand wiggled under my shirt, rolling down my stomach. When it gets lower, I try to buck my hips up toward him. The binds are around my hands, so I have some ability to lift up with my feet.

"Ah, not yet. I need to savor every moment so I can bear the in-between without your touch." Slowly he pulled off my clothes as if refusing to let anything else touch me beside him.

Finally, his hand brushed alongside the one thing that's most desperately aching for his touch. His hands almost feel soft in comparison to how ready I am for anything he could do. I strained against the restraints, letting them dig into my skin and pull my mind back along with it.

"We've been tied together since the day we met. I can see all those strings of fate now." His hands are along my thighs, but his focus is elsewhere on a binding I can't seem to see.

"Truly?"

Autar nodded. "Quite literally at times. If I'm not paying attention, almost forget that they are different from these at all."

"Different how?"

"When my hand touches one," Autar said, hand roaming back up and making me whine over the feeling. "It's like a lullaby."

I have no idea how I'm meant to reply to that, but Autar doesn't let me either. Dropping down and taking me in his mouth as his hands gripped tight on my hips. Filling my body with so much pleasure it's spilling out of my mouth as nothing but moans or his name.

After squeezing every golden second out of the hour, we untangle from the ropes and each other. Needing a moment apart to catch my breath and feel like a separate being again.

Autar's form had a lazy haze to it, that was growing more unfocused.

"Come on, look lively," I ordered.

"Why? Where are we going?"

"Got a few more favors to do."

Part Three: Grim Beasts
Chapter Twenty

Fearing we will get out right lost in these woods, I stopped. "Wait, why are we trying to go about this normally? We aren't normal. I *wish* we had something that could lead the way."

"Certainly, Master," Autar replied, and stretched his arms out. His wrists rotate up, then slowly pulled back as if drawing the wind close. "I found the Beast."

It's his voice speaking, but it's not quite him talking. Or at least not fully. The wish seemed filtered through magic. They are, and aren't, the same thing at times. But his panic over this duality doesn't return, so I believe we can handle whatever's ahead.

"After great falls, all of his men and all of his horses know the wolf calls," Autar said in rhyme.

"Are we in danger?"

The concept of *we* seemed to bring just Autar to the forefront. "Not if together again."

Wait… what? He actually still sounded like a nursery tale

I hadn't learned. "You in there?"

Autar rubbed at his eyes, then shook himself for good measure. He seems less comfortable, but more in his own, well, not skin, *form*. "Magic truly rattles shit around in your head."

"I'm glad you're okay."

"Better than ever," he smiled for a moment before the joy wavered. "There's something I reminded myself of. Can I ask why you used the safe word before?" The question is out of the blue, but I'm not even given a chance to reply as he continued. "I'm not upset. That's what it's there for. I just don't know exactly what happened days ago."

"I don't know…" Did I know? *Shit,* it's hard to look back and explain panic.

"May I guess?"

"Okay."

"Was the talk of forever too much? I didn't mean to bring up 'being together' like that."

"Am I that obvious, or were you thinking of it too?"

"Bit of both." He raised a single hand to shrug. "Hadi, it's fine. I'm not going to pressure you. Just trying to enjoy."

"Enjoy what?" His sentence ended short, but I need to hear the end of it.

Autar nervously laughed. "I'm trying not to make you anxious."

"May I guess? Are the missing words about being with me? Because that sounds like relationship talk?"

He nodded softly.

"What if I was wrong before?" I asked. "Maybe I did run away from things because that was easier than admitting that

I wanted to show you favor. That your life meant the most to me. It felt so wrong when I was meant to be unbiased."

"But now it's just us?"

I nodded. There were others somewhere close by. We might win some of their favor, others would probably always want us dead. "It's not a wish, not a command, just an ask. Take me back? I know I don't deserve another shot."

"Deserve?" He said harshly, cutting my plea off. "When has life ever been about what we deserve? Or want? Or even need? It's about holding on to that matters to us." He's looking over my face with a bobble of his head. "I've never let you go."

There's that flutter in my stomach, but this time I'm not afraid. "I'm in love with you so fucking much."

"Okay, calm down. We've been dating again for like three seconds," Autar laughed. "I fucking love you too. Let's go."

I worried the moment wasn't enough, but for the next bit we keep smiling at each other and how could I ever want for more?

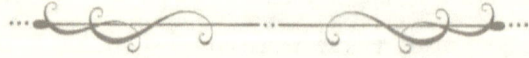

I had been too cautious about admitting what I wanted before I had the ability to have wishes granted. It was an anxious habit that carried over when now Autar could give me literally anything. But maybe this was the one time I should have thought things fully out first.

Magic must have its own scene of humor because we quickly came upon a couple of chariots that would quickly bring us to the Wolf King. Even before Prince Adam made it there. I was absolutely certain of this because all those men were still using all their horses. It was easy to tell how the Prince got the Beast nickname. The curling horns on his head suggested nothing else.

"It's the jinn!" a chariot driver yelled. He pulled on the reigns and brought the horses to a sudden stop in front of us. Made a bleak bit of sense we'd run into each other on the same path needed to find the same person.

After the assassination attempt, they must have returned to their original 'more noble' quest of returning the king to the empty throne until we presented them with a golden opportunity.

Without my sword, the fight devolved into a brawl. Prince Adam backed out of the fray letting his men fight. Seemed a coward's move until he started playing his violin. The melody boosted his men's actions as if bewitched. Made them stronger and faster under a shared hymn.

"Let me help!" Autar yelled to me over the fighting. He also had pulled back from the fight to avoid strangers grabbing at him, only to phase through him like a ghost.

"Stop the Beast," I ordered, struggling through the fight to even give him that much. "Flee if safer." If they wanted Autar, they'd still have to go through me first.

"Yes, Master," he replied sounding all too pleased.

The Prince's violin bow wavered. I would have thought it was because as a mage he could see a pissed-off jinn coming towards him. But his gaze was on me. "He's yours?"

There was a crack against my back, and I stumbled forward from the attack, breaking the eye contact. The wind picked up as Autar advanced and the Beast's attention was also stolen away as anything light enough to blow in the wind gets thrown around as fog rolls in.

"I had no idea!" Prince Adam yelled over everything.

The hurricane-force winds pushed the man who swung at me off balance, and I took the opportunity to knock the sword out of his hand. Another of the Prince's men charged at me. I brandish the fallen weapon. And he stops just short of impaling himself, sliding into a heap under the blade.

I tilted the sword down towards his throat. "Is this how you want to die?"

The man shook his head and slowly backed up. When he gained enough footing to stand, he only dared to grab his fellow fighter's shirt and pulled him away as well. *Respectable*.

"You tried to take me like I was a *thing*," Autar yelled over the storm. "Away from the people I care about."

I turned towards them and found the Beast on the ground. Musical instrument got further away as he crawled backward, eyes locked on Autar. "If anything, I thought I was being of assistance," he claimed. "Trying to free you!"

"No, you weren't," Autar growled.

My anger struck against my chest like a match. Both foreign, and completely mine. We'd been safe because I learned to trust those two mages. But too easily, I could have been stubborn and paid the price. *We* could have. I was Autar's master, but he was no one's slave.

"Make his bite as bad as his bark," I wished, fearing nothing. Not even whatever twist the magic made as the sky darkened.

A crack of lightning hit the Beast. A red fern leaf pattern raced across his skin, and thick hair quickly grew in its stead. When the magic touched his already animalistic features, they too grew grim. Fingernails growing into claws, teeth turning sharp, and extending past his mouth.

"Sic them," Autar ordered.

The Beast strained, trying to resist the command.

Howling an objection before his human mind seemed lost. With a growl, he was nothing more than a wild animal that charged at his men.

"The danger is over," I yelled. "Stop this!"

Autar watched as the animal snapped at the feet of his comrades. With a yelp, the animal jerked back as if on a leash, barely saved from taking a limb.

"You were so good, habib," I soothed. "You listen so well."

I think Autar would prefer killing them. The kindness doesn't win him over completely, but the anger in his jaw lessens at my words. "What now?"

"We take what we need and warn the Wolf King as asked."

He nodded and stepped up on a chariot, taking the reins for himself. I trailed a step behind, watching the animal dig in the back of their caravan for something. Food, maybe?

Glass shattered, and I watched the Beast drop back to the ground with a rose between his teeth. How the flower avoids being crushed is equally a miracle as everything else.

"Can we go?" Autar impatiently asked. To avoid causing further annoyance I jumped on and have the horses show us the way.

If it came down to Autar and me versus anyone else in the world. I'm choosing us. Every single time. That doesn't mean I am free of the guilt that comes along with those choices. Autar had never been that unhinged or yearning for revenge before. *What have I done?*

"Over 400 people died under your command," Autar said, far too casually for such a horrible thing. "Not sure why a few injuries of people attacking us would upset you now."

"You've been keeping track?"

"No," he said, with a tilt of his head. "Not then."

It's such a vague reply that I want to throttle him. "Pull over."

"What—why?"

"Pull over." He may control the horses, but I control him, and I feel him tugging back as if keeping both reins away from me. I grabbed them, and it's not even clear to me which set as Autar released control. We swerve, coming to a bouncy, hard stop against a tree.

Autar's hand grabbed his chest. But physically, we are both fine. Mentally? I think I snapped something in him. Maybe inside of us both, as I practically fell out of the carriage before making my way deeper into the forest. *We were warned that transmutation had a heavy cost...*

I know I don't go far, but not looking back makes it feel like enough to where I can breathe again. My eyes failed to keep focus on the forest ahead of me as I collapsed on the grass. Ahead was just a dark void, leaving the trees mere shadows of themselves in between the shadowy fog.

"Careful," Autar says, placing a hand on my shoulder and holding me back.

"Don't touch me!" His touch feels wrong. It's not the time for it, and I sweat even as I freeze.

His eyes aren't on me as I yell, transfixed to the blackness up ahead of us. He refused to pull away until I forced myself up to my feet and move to change that fact. "The buck always stops with me. I'm the one who is responsible."

Autar isn't listening and somehow that pissed me off further. "You think you can love me into reform?" I screamed. The thoughts felt like poison, but I can't stop them because they are coming from within me. "I'm a failure. I can't be saved or redeemed! Leave me be!"

Autar's attention shifted, but it wasn't to disagree. His eyes narrowed as he watched the surrounding ground.

"Why aren't you speaking to me?" My voice sounded broken, and I looked down, wondering if I'd be able to see the answer. There are multiple shadows. One followed the sun, the other stretches out from the darkness behind me.

A stabbing cold cascaded over my spine. When Autar finally looked directly at me, his eyes weren't his. They are solid black as whatever crept behind me engulfed me whole.

My back arched against the grass, and I don't even know how I'm on the ground, body thrashing out of my control. My lungs don't even release the air I need to call for help.

My life flashed before my eyes. Each memory feels like it's being torn out from my mind like a page in a book. My hand reached out to grasp anything… and I hear Autar's voice.

"Habib." His voice is a cool breeze as I burned up. "Forgive yourself and let me in… Yes, you can. Trust me."

I always have. Often more than I've trusted myself. Just when I feel like I'm going to shake apart, Autar filled my senses as the sky swims back to me. Within the first exhale, the word sorry passes between my lips. For everyone I've let down in my life, and for the first time, that includes myself.

As I pushed myself up, there was a smoky before and after image to my motions. I took an extra moment to wave my hand about, to make sure I'm seeing what I think I am. "Autar? This you?"

It doesn't just feel around me, but between my skin, blood, and bones, holding it all together. It feels… loving. My body also ached, like it was not fully mine. Hurt in the areas that I used to see Autar babying on his worst days.

This… possession felt more like walking in someone else's shoes.

"We need to go deeper," I heard myself say. It's my fear that's holding us back again. "I know you're scared, but the right path is this way."

Together as a single being the shadowy magical barrier moves over us like oil over water.

The glint of sunlight returned, revealing a clearing in the surrounding forest. A meadow with wildflowers line the edge where a cabin sat just off our path. For such isolation, there's a well-kept porch and the smell of meat cooking over a fire inside.

Autar pulled free from me, and emotion seized me to the point of physical pain. At first, I wondered if this was how he felt every time I pushed him away. I double over at the weight of it all, gritting my teeth and unable to hold back the dam of what is own share of the pain that I refused to feel.

"You okay?" Autar asked, as I lifted my head enough to see his boots. "I know you didn't mean those things. Or rather, I know it was self-loathing talking."

"How?" Tears fell onto the grass below. I desperately wanted to be in control of my own body again.

"Your guilt, the wish, all of those broken pieces drew us here, but the barrier attacks ill-intent and utterly rejects all non-magical things."

If he isn't angry with me, I can try to not be upset with myself either as I stand. "Where is here?"

Autar squinted over at me as if I lost my marbles on the other side. "You don't know?"

Chapter Twenty-One

An arrow cut across the air, and I pulled back, realizing afterward it was a warning shot. "You can't have him!" yelled a man in a green-hooded tunic. "Return to wherever you came from."

Autar took a step forward, his hands out and low. "The Mad Hatter sent us."

"I'm not returning the coin." The runes on the archer's bow glowed as he released another shot. Surely expecting the arrow to phase through him, Autar didn't retreat. The arrow bit into his shoulder. Taking a wisp of smoke, and a spurt of blood with it.

More deep red trickled down his arm as Autar just stared in surprise. "I can bleed?"

The archer notched another arrow and I put my body in front of Autar's. "Wait! Please, we are lost and need help."

The man hesitated as the door to the cottage opened behind him.

"Robin, I'm okay." This man had silver hair that looked black underneath, like a wolf's pelt. And if that wasn't unique enough, the matching animal followed him out. No doubt this was the Wolf King. "It was his own demons that didn't let him in. They mean us no harm."

"Which one, Mal?" Robin said, trying to look past me.

"Mine!" I said, taking another step closer and being glad for once in my life that I could admit that. "I'm the fuck up that was bottling everything up." I carefully gestured towards Autar behind me. "His magic was just protecting me from myself."

Robin looked back to Mal, who nodded an agreement, before slowly lowering his bow. I gave it a careful second, before rushing back to Autar, my hand now pressed over his wound. "How did this happen? Is it because you were one with me?"

Autar shook his head, pointing up with his other hand. "It's golden hour."

"What? It was midday not five minutes ago." I glanced up at the setting sun hanging high on the horizon.

"This is a pocket of Neverland," the former king said, and started to walk over, hands in his pockets. The wolf decided to stay behind, resting his head on its paws. "It's whatever time I like."

I peeled my hand away from Autar's wound, giving Mal a careful glance as he stepped closer. Autar was still bleeding. "Can your magic heal?"

"Come inside," Robin said. "I'll patch him up."

"You can't. Only I'm meant to touch him." Realizing too late that I sounded extremely jealous over even the idea of another man touching him.

Thankfully, Mal didn't push the subject, just blinked. "Okay, you then."

"I can fix me," Autar grumbled. "I'm jinn, not a broken

toy needing stitches."

Mal smiled and started walking back to the cabin. "You shot a genie."

"A what?" Robin asked, glancing back towards Autar. "I thought those were extinct."

"Hadi thought you were a just story," he countered.

Somehow, that seemed to surprise Robin most of all. "That was in question?"

"To some," Autar added. "Believe I exist like this because I was blessed by the Hatter."

The wolf's ears perked up and growled quietly. Gave me the suspicion that this once and nevermore king had been 'blessed' as well. "How is that mad man?" Mal asked.

"Ran away to wed the Frog Prince," I answered.

The man froze halfway up the trio of steps to the cabin before he laughed. "Okay, I want to hear that story."

I explained what I know about the state of the Wonderland since their disappearance while Autar is holding pressure over the wound with clean rags Mal gave him.

"Sorry about firing on you," Robin said, still not looking forgiven enough through Autar is not upset. "Before we came here, someone tried to summon Mal away. And I thought…" He shook his head, cutting himself off. "Doesn't matter."

"Can't say I blame you," Autar said, glancing to me and I knew he wanted to tell him about the Beast. When I don't interrupt, he continued. "We too might have gotten overzealous and turned the Beast into an actual animal."

"You did what?" Mal replied harshly.

Shit, were they friends?

"Henri and Madison told us to find you because he was originally searching for you," I explained, waiting a beat to see how he'd handle this news before moving on as quickly as possible. "Then the Beast's plans changed, wanted his own jinn and set out to separate Autar and me. Magic isn't natural to us, so I can't claim we know what we are doing with it."

"That's enough politics at our table," Robin said softly, hand rubbing over Mal's shoulders. "All sounds very stressful, and we are not willing to judge how you protect each other."

Mal nodded an agreement but looked like he'd need longer to properly process it all.

"We might have dice somewhere if you'd like a play a game while I finish up with our meal?" Robin offered.

"I have a deck of cards handy," I said and pulled my bag up onto to table.

"Really?" Robin asked. "Can't say either of us has played with them since we were children. Became too tied to the Queen of Hearts herself as adults. Just like how one stops playing with wooden soldiers once war is no longer pretend."

"We'd be happy to show you how?" Autar offered.

There weren't enough seats for the four of us, so Robin carefully balanced on the wooden arm of Mal's chair. "What do you think?"

"Sounds good."

We all played several rounds of a game they remembered. When we changed games, Robin stepped out to get more firewood while Mal asked to watch to learn the rules of the new one.

"Queen's first club," I said, with a grin as I placed the ten of clubs down next to my queen of the same suit.

"A card so violent," whispered Mal, and went ignored as Autar disregarded us both and flipped over a red queen for himself. "I'm sorry, what were we talking about?"

I glanced to Autar to silently ask if I was the one mishearing things.

"He's just trying to bluff that he'll get a flush," Autar explained on my behalf, but his kind expression seemed lost on Mal. I wasn't even sure he was truly looking at the cards anymore.

There was a scratching on the door as the wolf pawed at the wooden frame, asking to be let out. When it didn't instantly open, the wolf whined. That sound was enough to get Mal moving. "If you'll excuse me," he said, as he opened the door to let the animal out.

"That was strange," Autar said after the door closed from its own weight behind Mal.

I struggled. "Would you please draw? It's your turn."

"Angry, and senseless," Autar said somberly as he drew a card. "No one will question their new Red Queen."

Now I slowed the game down as I just stared over at him. "What in all the stars are you going on about?"

"It's what Mal said," Autar explained with a frown as he reorganized his hand of cards. "I thought if I repeated the phrase, it would make sense."

"In no way whatsoever did he say all of that." I threw my hand in after pulling a two of hearts and ruining my flush.

"Yes, he did," Autar insisted, looking at me as if I was crazy. "After 'a card so violent' while he was staring off?"

"I mean this in the nicest way possible," I said and gathered all the cards to shuffle. "You are hearing things."

"You positive?"

I nodded and dealt another hand of five out to us both. This time I started with two pairs. Much better.

Or so I thought until Autar's gaze was angled out the window as if to see where our hosts had gone. "I don't think he's well."

"Maybe that's why he's not king anymore." I gestured for him to pick up the cards. "Are you playing?"

"Oh, sorry." Autar looked over his at hand, frowning.

Telling myself it was because it was a bad hand, or that he was bluffing, would have been easier. This conversation would end here. But I didn't want things to just end between us anymore. "Good thing they have each other?"

Autar smiled a little. "Yeah, you're right there."

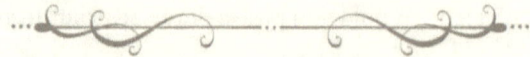

I waited until after dinner to explain our new cause. "So if you do the transmutation, the Prince can return to himself."

"Look, I'm sympathetic to your cause. I have Polaris because of the Beast," Mal said tightly. "But I don't do saving anymore. It's not that I don't know how, more…"

Polaris interrupted him by dragging his food bowl across

the floor. The metal scrapping loudly continued as his snout pushed at it.

"Would you leave it?" Mal groaned. The wolf laid down, large eyes pouting. "I'm sorry, but my magic isn't for others. And if that makes me selfish, so be it."

"Could you at least teach us how?" I asked. Surely that was a reasonable compromise.

"Not now," Robin insisted, and we shut up quick. "Mal, please. You're ignoring your dog." Robin cited as if it was a domestic pet, instead of a hundred-pound wild animal.

"He wants to hunt," Mal huffed, and the wolf got up to his feet as if in agreement. "We are going outside."

He left as Autar and I just stood there, knowing we weren't any closer to the answers we wanted.

"Is there game out there?" Autar asked.

Robin nodded. "Nature seems to have its own magic. The barrier seems to only affect things capable of speech."

I sat down, wondering if the Beast would now apply or not, causing my guilt to only grow. It was Autar's magic, but I'm the one who gave the order. The sooner we fixed this the better. "I'm going to step out too."

As I explored a faintly beaten path, a rocky shoreline appeared. The lake isn't large enough for waves, but the wind rippled across the water's surface.

I heard a whisper of a step behind me and turned. Barely avoiding an ethereal blade that's held out towards my throat. Mal stands on the other side. Normally I can't see when a mage is casting, but Mal is so full of the dark chaotic swirl his eyes are black pools, accented by glowing runes on his skin. *He must be the one who created the buffer between himself and the rest of Wonderland.*

"This is my forest," he said. "I will not be your prey."

171

"I'm not here to hunt you." My hands rose to help prove it. "Once we can get your help, we will go."

"I don't see a difference."

My jaw moved to speak, but I'm cut off.

"I said, no. I will not let you turn me into another animal." It's the way he says it that ran a chill up my spine. "Autar said you were different. That you respected no," Mal continued, finally pulling the blade back, and it vanished from sight with a shimmer. "I don't believe him."

When did they have the chance to talk privately? Does their magic communicate to each other? It didn't matter anyway, since questions got me further away from what we needed. "How can I prove it to you?"

"Ask someone else."

"There's only you. You're the only one who can control transmutation."

"There's always someone else." Mal's gaze lowered to the ground as Polaris stood behind him. The animal's sharp eyes tracked me as he paced. "You have my answer. Do what you will. I'm going home to Robin."

I let him go ahead before I frankly started following again. My intent to continue this conversation was seemingly too well-known as I opened the cabin door.

"I'm not the only one who can control transmutation," Mal near repeated before his head turned from me to Autar. "You already have everything you need. It's time to realize that."

"Me?" Autar asked.

"A while back, before I set up the boundary, I was summoned against my will. Brought into a room of smoke and pain where a man aimed to siphon my magic so he could do feats he was not capable of himself. That's what these marks do," Mal said and pulled up his sleeve as if we hadn't already caught them before. Now dull and faded to black. "They let magic in but can be twisted. *Tapped.* A genie and their master must work similarly. One wishes, and the magic within the other rises to the call. Autar isn't harmed in the process because you have his trust."

"You have our respect for how far you came," Robin added diplomatically, "but you do not have our trust. Therefore, we cannot help you in this manner."

"That makes our bond sound equally problematic," I countered.

"Is it?" Mal asked.

"Could you break it?" I'm not sure why the hypothetical matters to me, but I suddenly does. *Deeply.*

"Why would I?"

No wonder he didn't stay ruler for long, probably made a host of enemies quickly. "It's what a king should do."

"Hadi, stop," Autar mumbled.

Mal looked bored as he spoke. "Shame for your self-sabotaging that you didn't find me when I was king then."

"I thought Robin Hood's whole thing was helping people in need."

Robin set the pan he was cooking with down suddenly, and it sizzled on the countertop. "He asked you why?"

"Excuse me?"

I looked over at Autar for help, but he was evasive, as Robin spoke again. "Do you find your arrangement unfair?"

"...No." Autar's words were nearly silent as he fidgeted with the deck of cards on the table. They were stacked unevenly, but he didn't seem able to topple them despite the prodding.

"See," Robin said. "No issue here, so why you are making problems for yourself?"

Maybe I was being an ass. "You sound like the Hatter."

Mal's bristled. "Sometimes… Madison is right about what's best." The fact that it seemed hard for him to admit that made me believe it's truer than I could imagine. "You can stay until you are fit to leave, but only because I feel as if my wards set you back."

"Why do you think that?"

Mal stood up, and his wolf growled while its yellow eyes stay locked on me. "Because I don't see what Autar could see in you otherwise." When he's done speaking, he casually walked into the other room as if it's not the cruelest thing anyone could ever have uttered aloud to me.

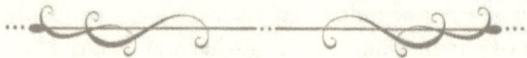

Night fell, and unable to sleep, I stared out the window at the fireflies outside. They seem so bright before something much sharper flickered into existence. Autar is out there somewhere. I knew I ran him off with my comments, but I don't think the lights were from him.

Worried I may have caught the start of a forest fire, I grabbed my bag and headed outside. The initial fear is replaced with a heavy feeling in my stomach as there are burn lines in the grass.

Slowly, I follow the concentric circles towards the center where I find Mal sitting.

"How do you do that?"

His legs were crossed as if meditating. The wolf isn't with him, so must be sleeping back at the cabin with Robin.

"Do what?"

"Come back to yourself? After…" *What was I even trying to ask?* If I didn't know, how was he meant to answer me? I always wanted to blame magic itself, but that's not what makes me feel a kinship towards him. He'd seen war. "Everything you've been through."

"You feel it, endure it, best you can." His eyes looked up at the night sky. Maybe even at the one he named his wolf after, as a couple of shooting stars dart across. "That's the only way it ever lets go of you. Afterward, it's a controlled burn."

I fell silent, taking up enough of his time already. He was right. I was better than I was being. Old habits die so hard. I hadn't wished to be perfect. Learning to cope in a new way just gave me the chance at a better tomorrow.

"Robin is used to living with a group of people," he continued. "He doesn't outright say it, but I know it's been lonely at times, living like this. I'm the happiest I've ever been, and it's still on even me hard sometimes."

I don't know how or why he's confiding in me suddenly. Being close to royalty, keeping their secrets is something I've done since I can remember. But this isn't that. It's more… honest.

"So tell me," Mal continued, "do you honestly want to break what's tying you and Autar together?"

"Felt like I should," I confessed. It was selfish to keep him. Refusing to return the lamp when Jasmine ordered me had been for Autar. It seemed like a fate worse than death. Now? If we could safely and cleanly separate our lives from each other, *I* didn't want to. If Autar wanted to stay, how was it selfish?

"Are you realizing why life doesn't work solely off 'should'?" Mal asked, as his hand moved to his chest to the coin on his necklace. It's in this moment I see why the Royals of Heart chose him to rule. Wonderland might be better for him still preceding over it. But he wouldn't be better for it.

"Because I'm the one living it?" I answered, laughing at myself a bit. Felt so simple now. As obvious as the sun rising along with daybreak.

Mal smiled. After a moment, he held his hand up. And I step forward, grabbing it and helping him up. He placed a hand on my shoulder, and we walk back to his house in silence.

I sit there on the porch until the next golden hour. Time here is strange. If Mal does control it, seemed unconsciously so. But I don't need to figure it out to make the best of it.

Autar hasn't returned, and instead of trying to summon him out of wherever he's gone, I walked around hoping to find him. A short way back from the barrier, I see him.

"I never actually asked what you wanted," I called.

Autar turned towards me, still looking confused and hurt. And I could never blame him for that.

"Sorry, I've been an ass," I said, moving closer. "What do you want? Today. Tomorrow. Years from now. I've been trying to do right by you, without ever asking what you defined as 'right'. There's no more rule book."

He smiled a little, speaking softly against the gentle swish of grass. "There certainly isn't."

"What do you want?"

His eyes held mine for a moment before falling to the center of my chest. After a step closer, he spread his hand across the embroidered tree, fingers stretching out among the branches.

Pink petals lift off the tree's image. They look

remarkably soft as the wind lifted their growing number into the air. Autar smiled to himself before opening his eyes and enjoying his work around us. "I want to see a whole new world," he said, as he caught an impossibly pink petal between his fingers.

"What are these from?" This feels like a dream, their colors off from our waking world.

"No tree I know, but it's what I see when I let myself want a future," he said, letting the wind carry the burst of color away.

"Sounds beautiful." I'm not sure if I'm talking about the petals, the future, or being together. But it doesn't matter as he pulled me near, catching me between his lips and he's the most gorgeous one of them all.

"Stop letting me go," he whispered against my mouth.

"Never again, I promise." *And what is a vow if not a wish?*

The sky is aglow with shooting stars now, so bright that I advert my eyes. It's as if I'm falling and hit the ground while still in my bed.

Only to wake up somewhere else...

"Autar." The name is a gasp on my lips. All I'm sure of is that we are somewhere else, closer to home. There are sand dunes as far as I can see.

My bag's strap isn't looped around me, so I dig my hands into the sand to search for the lamp. *I can't lose him.* Won't ever let go without reaching instantly back out.

There's metal under my fingertips and I pulled up the lamp, rubbing the surface feverishly. No smoke rose, but I refuse to stop until there's a spark of magic inside. There's no such thing as a final wish. *We have more...*

"I love seeing you worry about me," Autar teased. He's standing a few feet away with a smirk on his face. "All panicked and concerned. Openly too. Someone will surely accuse you of favoritism now."

"Asshole! You *are* my favorite." I hurled the lamp at him, but it just shimmers through him.

"Yeah," he added smugly and stepped over the lamp. "I know. Where to, Master?"

"How am I supposed to know? You're the one who teleported us!"

"Nuh-uh," Autar tsked. "The magic needs us both."

Any attempt to stand is thrown off as my eyes stay glued to the lamp. "Don't we need that? Why can't you touch it anymore?" These rules have a strange fluid, almost living, consent to them.

"It's empty of magic. I am free of the knot that tied me to it." His hand moved over his heart. "It's all here now. Neither we, nor I, need anything else."

I fell back onto the sand. The sky is so stark with white clouds, and I blinked up at the brightness. "Was scaring me necessary?"

Autar sat down near me. "Maybe not."

I rolled my head towards him. His focus is on Agrabah's skyline, but I can't imagine anything better than what's already in front of me. And I don't think he meant to alarm either, just a funny accident. "Do you enjoy tormenting me at least?"

He grinned. "Come on, look lively."

"Why? Where are we going?"

"Got a few more sins to atone for."

Chapter Twenty-Two

Autar couldn't be taken from me. Our destiny was still tied together. I could summon him if I called, but there was no physical object that could be stolen out from under us. It meant we could track down the Beast without fear. We'd be safe and unstoppable.

I watched as the lamp sank into the desert. Autar swirled his hands around and created a whirlpool that pulled the lamp deep within the sea of sand.

To be honest, I'd miss the lamp. For all the trouble it caused me, I'd grown fond of it. It had brought us back together. If someone else needed it in the future, I hoped it would be found again.

"There's somewhere else we need to be," Autar said, as he moved closer to me.

As much as I enjoyed it, I don't understand why. "What are you doing?"

"Focus on that sin again." He smirked as his eyes caught mine as his dark gaze sent a pool of desire through me. "Babe, touching me isn't a sin. Concentrate on the regret."

"Prince Adam." The name tumbled from my thoughts and Autar nodded. "He's still a beast."

"I think I can use your shadow to travel to him," Autar added, carefully stepping into my silhouette, which glistens with his presence.

If I had a weaker stomach, the contents of it would have been thrown up as the world titled upside with a swoosh. This was different from how we moved before, but this place wasn't new.

The Beast was here, corralled into the tight streets that we'd been hiding in. No one saw him as the royal he truly was.

There's a warning growl for the people between us and him. I recognized Nonya and Ruthie as part of the crowd holding him back. For better or worse, they seemed on the same side now. Ruthie was perceptive enough that she spotted us over her shoulder. Sword not lowering but resolve lessening.

"Focus," Nonya scolded.

"Look who it is," Ruthie replied, and tilted our direction so the sword stayed pointed towards the cornered animal.

"Let us fix this." I walked up to the group and Ruthie stepped back to let Autar and me in front. My movements slowed in front of the animal. The rose was still between the snarling animalistic mouth. If people had just taken a moment without fear, they'd realized this was all an injury they didn't understand.

Autar's hands were at his side as sand started to rise, ready to pull whatever else he may need from the ground. "We wish to undo what has been done to you."

The grains swirled until the Beast was encircled in the sandstorm. There's a clear version of what I want to happen here, but…

"Shit, how do mages do this so easily?" Autar asked, teeth gritted as the animal's jaws snap at the magic.

As if to fulfill his wish of an answer, a memory came to me. There was a path in the courtyard, where flowers were repeatedly trampled. Everyone kept crossing over them to save a few steps. Even the gardener, if in a hurry.

"It's a desire path." This realization makes having control of magic, *at all*, even more impressive. I shouldn't have feared mages for being able to do magic. I should have marveled at their willpower. "Let the magic flow how it wants."

Autar's eyes flared gold at the permission and the swirling tide gains a bit of his murky color. With a whine, the creature stumbled forward. Paws unfurled with a crack of bone as hands push him up to stand like a man. The rose falls from his mouth as the teeth retract.

"There's something inside of him and isn't allowing me to fix this how we see it," Autar said, straining.

"Then stop," I commanded, and Autar pulled free. His smoky form whipped back from the gust before settling back into shape. "We can't fix what he wants broken."

Each second that passed, the beast looked more like the Prince. The first thing he does as a person is reach for the fallen flower on the ground.

I stepped closer, giving him an extra moment before his wearily gaze lifted to me. "Seems that's the best we can do for you. If you need anything more find that wolf you created. Don't ask for their return. Don't ask for anything. They'll give you everything you need."

Autar watched the man, expression darker, as if still uncertain of his true worth.

"Come on," I said, "We're done here."

Chapter Twenty-Three

Do you think you would grant me a wish for each shooting star we see tonight?" I asked as we watched the sky.

Autar stayed silent as if to first count. "What were we thinking with only three wishes? Caused so much strife and worry."

"We know better now."

"Do we think we can change them?" Autar asked watching as lines of light streak past.

"The stars?" He nodded before we both fell silent for a moment. "I think we already did and will continue to in whatever way we need to be happy together."

"We just need to follow our heart," Autar agreed with a nod, before his eyes suddenly widened. "You gave me an idea."

He took off afterward, and I could only run after him. "Wait up! What in all the lands did you suddenly think of?"

"Not in the lands," he said, stopping as inhumanly fast. "Not Wonderland. The sky. There's more out there."

ROSE SINCLAIR

A bright line of shimmering light streaked across the sky. It's beautiful, but I still don't understand. "Where, Autar?"

His smoke curled in frustration over not knowing where to start. "I don't think shadows are a natural way to travel. Or, at least, not for me."

"Okay?"

"I don't make a shadow, right?" Autar explained, and I glanced down as if to check. Not like there was enough sunlight to make one much of one right now anyway. "I grant wishes. Wish to move freely through the heavens."

There's a stray shooting star that is soon joined by several more of various sizes and brightness. And I find the moment truly magical. We really could do anything. "I find myself only wishing to right our wrongs and stay together. I love you, that will always be enough for me now."

Autar inhaled sharply. I reached out to steady him before realizing its futile, and instead hope my combination of words was alright.

"I love you too, you careless bastard," he laughed. "I need you to concentrate."

"I did promise you a whole new world. Should I wish for that?"

"No," he answered softly. "You never promised."

"What if I did now?"

He held his breath for a moment, and it looked like hope. "I'd like that."

This time, I don't wait for the sun. I placed my hand by his, spreading my fingers out to allow space for where his would go. Autar mirrored the gesture. I can't physically feel it, but where it matters in my heart, I do.

Slowly, I pull my hand up and he follows my lead until

our hands are under my lips where I kiss the air between us. "I promise and wish it, too."

Autar shivered as magic rolled through him. I hold on, tightening my fingers, and feel the buzz of magic against my rough hands.

He stepped forward, and I remain willfully tied to him as I follow. Autar walks us over to a ring of mushrooms in the grass. I think it's where he was originally leading us.

His hand reached over as magic pours out like pitcher of water. Flooding the area but somehow contained within the fairy ring. Once the water has any depth, I started to see more than just grass. Someplace new. "Where does that go?"

Autar pulled his free hand up and away, for being the one who had summoned it, he doesn't seem to have any more idea than I do. "Does it matter, as long as we're together?"

"As long as we are together and happy too."

His laugh lines deepen as he smiled. "Ever after."

ABOUT THE AUTHOR

Rose Sinclair is the profane community leader who started with a blog in 2013. The biggest noise maker they spearheaded was a protest in 2015 that made GLADD step up for the wider LGBTQIA+ community, paving the way for future acceptance for people and on-screen TV representation. Before becoming a full-time writer, they popularized several terms, and set up a decentralized support system with a "Dear Abby" style approach. They are the author of HELLO WORLD, the BIG BAD MAGIC fantasy romance series, and plenty of other queer love stories.

Don't forget to drop your email at RoseSinclair.com so you don't miss out any new releases and get exclusive free stories!

www.ingramcontent.com/pod-product-compliance
Lightning Source LLC
Chambersburg PA
CBHW051257250626
47155CB00009B/3324